TRANSFORMERS ADVENTURES
VOLUME 1

SCRIPT SIMON FURMAN

ARTISTS GEOFF SENIOR NICK ROCHE ANDREW WILDMAN
DON FIGUEROA GUIDO GUIDI MARCELO MATERE

TITAN BOOKS

VOLUME 1

ISBN-10: 1 84576 836 1
ISBN-13: 9781845768362

First published April 2008

2 4 6 8 10 9 7 5 3 1

Published by Titan Books, a division of Titan Publishing Group Ltd., 144 Southwark Street, London, SE1 0UP.

www.titanbooks.com

Please email us at: readerfeedback@titanemail.com

A CIP catalogue record for this title is available at the British Library

PRINTED IN SPAIN

WHO ARE THEY?

They're a race of sentient robots with the power to alter their physical forms.

WHERE ARE THEY FROM?

Cybertron – a planet of living metal. Its power source is the Allspark – a giant cube generating unimaginable amounts of energy.

IS CYBERTRON A PLACE I'D LIKE TO VISIT?

If you need scrap metal! Cybertron, once a place of great beauty, is now a badly damaged hulk, ravaged by the endless war between the Autobots and the Decepticons.

THE WHO AND THE WHAT?

The Autobots and the Decepticons – bottom line: the good guys and the bad guys. The Autobots believe in honour and justice, steered by the guiding light and awesome presence of Optimus Prime. The Decepticons have been twisted by the tyrannical leadership of Megatron, whose desire for the Allspark has driven him over the edge of sanity. Their war has left their home planet in ruins.

SO WHERE DOES THIS LEAVE THINGS?

Well, the war has gone badly for the Autobots and Megatron is close to finally seizing control of the Allspark. All that stands between him and the power to control the universe are six heroic Autobots…

TRANSFORMERS 101

CYBERTRON:
NO MATTER HOW MANY TIMES MEGATRON TRIES TO KILL ME, NO MATTER HOW MANY DRONES HE SENDS AT ME...
...I STUBBORNLY REFUSE TO DIE.
I'D GIVE MY OWN LIFE IN AN INSTANT, IF IT MEANT AN END TO THIS CARNAGE, BUT RIGHT NOW—FOR BETTER OR FOR WORSE—I AM THE ONLY THING STANDING BETWEEN MEGATRON...
OPTIMUS PRIME

SCRIPT SIMON FURMAN • **ART** GEOFF SENIOR • **COLOURS** ROBIN SMITH • **LETTERS** JIMMY BETANCOURT/COMICRAF

...AND THE ALLSPARK!
THE LIVING, BEATING HEART OF CYBERTRON, IT POSSESSES THE UNFATHOMABLE POWER TO CREATE... OR DESTROY.
IN MEGATRON'S HANDS...
...IT WOULD SURELY BE THE LATTER!
NOTHING WILL STOP HIM IN HIS SINGLE-MINDED DETERMINATION TO POSSESS IT – NOTHING. WHICH IS WHY, ULTIMATELY...
...I INTEND TO PUT THE ALLSPARK BEYOND HIS REACH ONCE AND FOR ALL!
MEGATRON'S FORCES ARE EVERYWHERE, SEARCHING, MY OWN WARRIORS DEPLOYED IN A DESPERATE ATTEMPT TO WAYLAY HIM.
ALL THAT REMAINS...

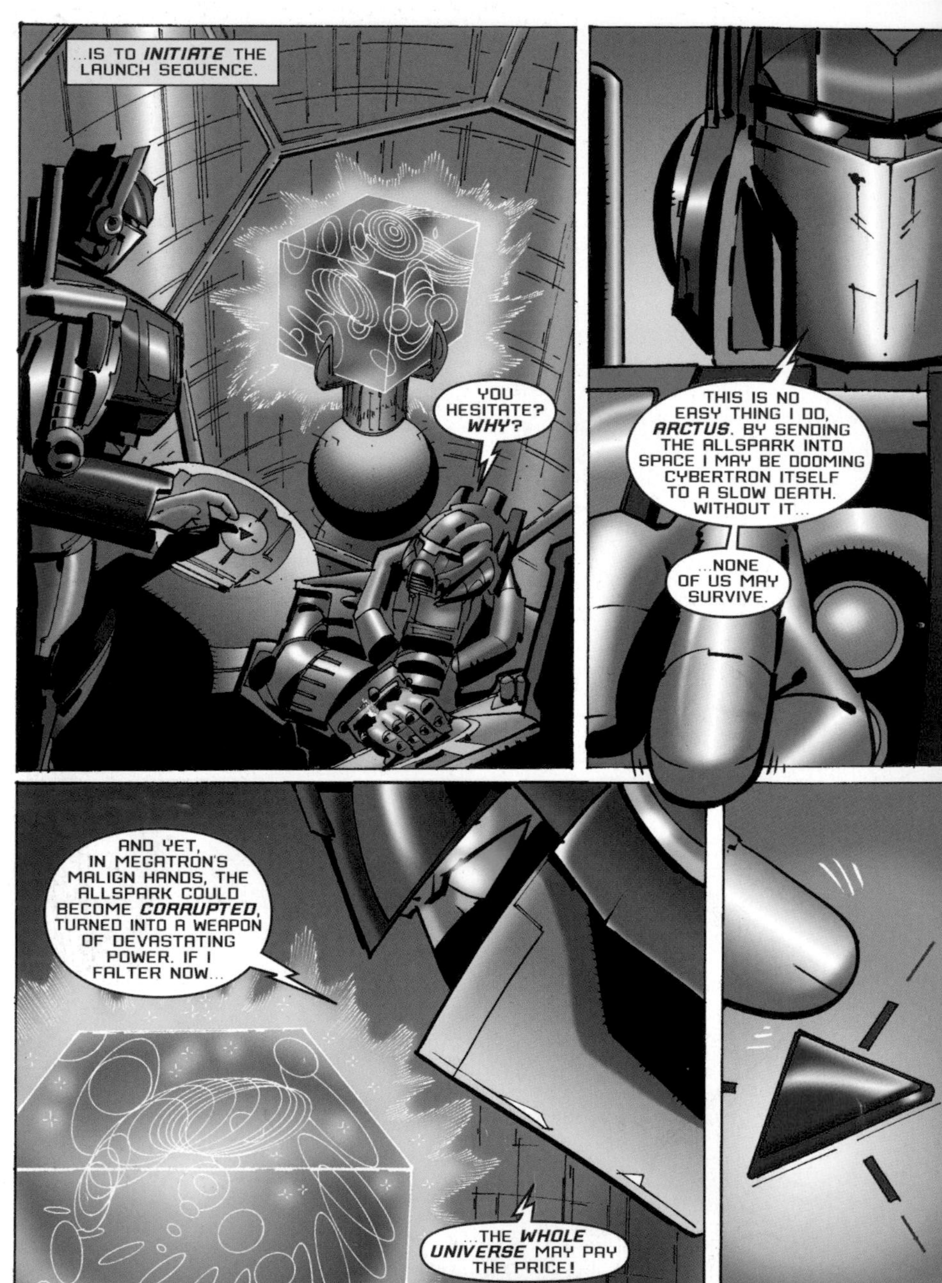
...IS TO INITIATE THE LAUNCH SEQUENCE.
YOU HESITATE? WHY?
THIS IS NO EASY THING I DO, ARCTUS. BY SENDING THE ALLSPARK INTO SPACE I MAY BE DOOMING CYBERTRON ITSELF TO A SLOW DEATH. WITHOUT IT...
...NONE OF US MAY SURVIVE.
AND YET, IN MEGATRON'S MALIGN HANDS, THE ALLSPARK COULD BECOME CORRUPTED, TURNED INTO A WEAPON OF DEVASTATING POWER. IF I FALTER NOW...
...THE WHOLE UNIVERSE MAY PAY THE PRICE!

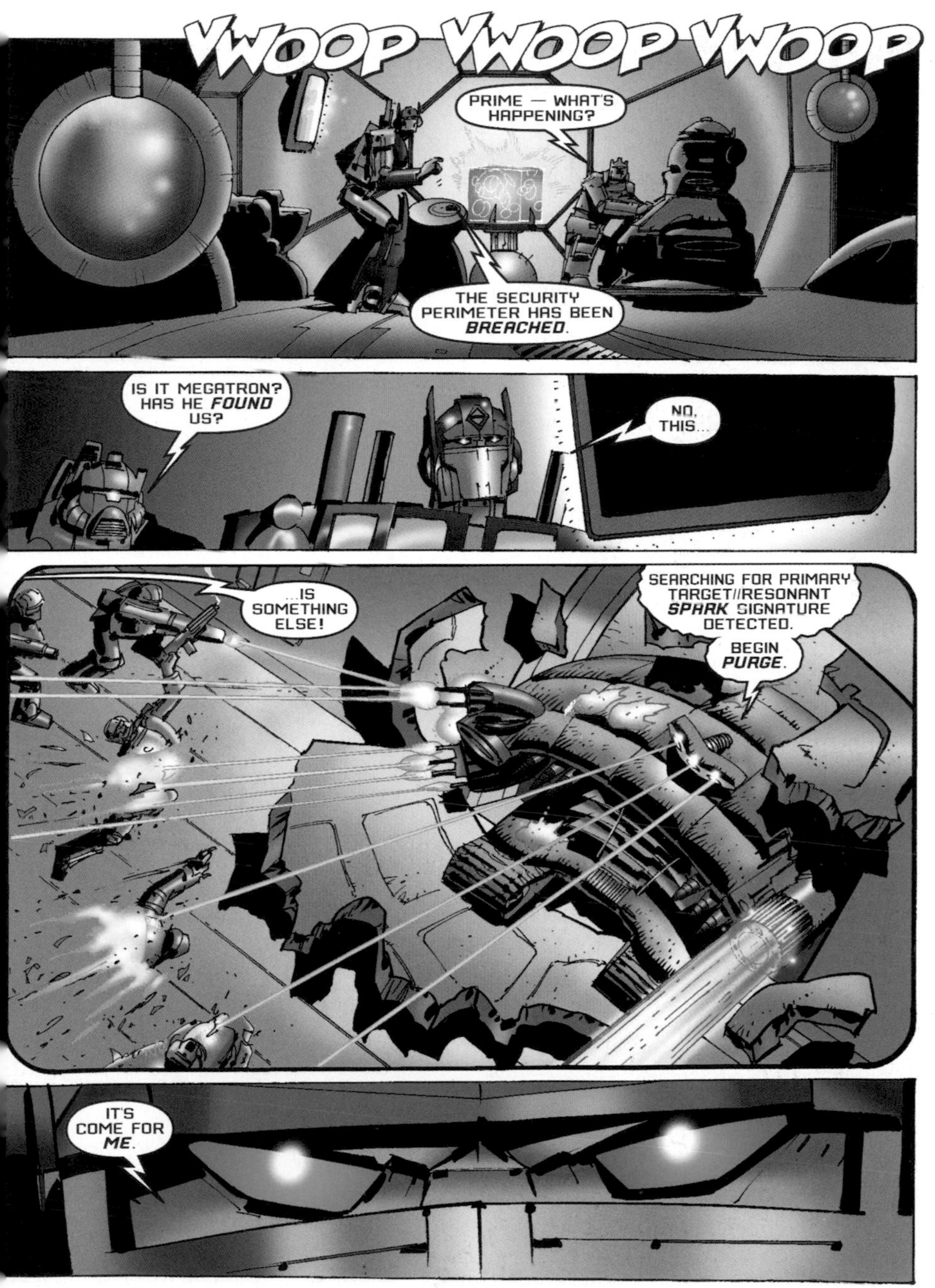

...IS SOMETHING ELSE!

SEARCHING FOR PRIMARY TARGET//RESONANT *SPARK* SIGNATURE DETECTED.

BEGIN *PURGE*.

WHAT? HOW CAN YOU *KNOW* THAT?
I JUST DO. I KNOW HOW MEGATRON THINKS. TAKE ME OUT OF THE EQUATION, THE *AUTOBOT* RESISTENCE CRUMBLES.
NO TIME TO HESITATE NOW. IF I'M NOT BACK IN TEN CYCLES...

"...*LAUNCH* THE ALLSPARK!"

THE DRONE WON'T STOP UNTIL IT HAS *FOUND* ME. MEGATRON MUST HAVE SOMEHOW ADAPTED IT TO ZERO IN ON THE UNIQUE *ENERGY MATRIX* WITHIN MY SPARK CORE.
NO POINT RUNNING, OR HIDING...

FWUSHH

VA VAAAM
...I NEED TO MEET THIS *HEAD-ON*!

PRIMARY TARGET...
...ACQUIRED!

TOO LATE I REALISE...

...IT WAS THE *WORST* THING I COULD HAVE DONE!

[*ZRT*] ALLSPARK DETECTED! DIRECTIVE OVERRIDE.

REFORMATTING PRIMARY MISSION OBJECTIVES...

I HAVE *MOMENTS* TO ACT...

...BEFORE THE DRONE REPORTS ITS FINDINGS AND LOCATION DIRECTLY TO MEGATRON.
NEVER TRIED THIS BEFORE, NOT IN SUCH AN ENCLOSED SPACE...
...BUT MY OPTIONS ARE SEVERELY LIMITED!
I HAVE TO END THIS...
VOOOOM
...NOW!

CHAAAANK
WITH MY LAST CONSCIOUS THOUGHT I...
...TRANSFORM...
THUNND
...
BUT...
...THERE IS *MORE* TO COME.

MUCH MORE!

OUR WAR... ON ANOTHER WORLD!

OPTIMUS PRIME

INTRODUCTION

Possessing power beyond easy measure, Optimus Prime is a study in contradictions. Wherever possible, Prime strives to employ reason over force, forever seeking peaceful solutions to conflicts. However, should reason fail, he can – and does – unleash a whole array of offensive options, using a staggering barrage of explosive, incendiary and concussive force against those who threaten life and liberty. In peacetime, Prime was a stoic and dignified head of state, and though now forced into his current role as reluctant warrior hero, those qualities still define him.

HISTORY

(ALL)SPARK TO FLAME

Megatron's attempts to control and subvert the almost limitless power of the sacred Allspark prompted Optimus Prime to gather a fighting force of his own. Prime knew that Megatron intended to turn the Allspark's life-giving powers into a dark source of anti-creation, through which he would ultimately rule the universe. Prime was willing to sacrifice his own life to stop Megatron, but he concluded it was better to simply put the Allspark beyond Megatron's reach forever... even though it might mean the end of Cybertron!

ROBOT MODE

- A unique sub-system of hyper-coil musculature makes him stronger than almost any Transformer.
- A cobalt super-alloy makes him highly resistant to impact or explosive damage.
- His spark (life essence) is a source of enormous energy, compacted to a core of intense fissionable matter.

WEAPONS MODE

Prime's primary weapon is his laser-sighted barrage cannon, which fires a cache of plutonium-tipped warheads, each with a maximum range of 60 miles and an explosive yield equivalent to 3000 lbs of TNT. It also features an auto-reloader, allowing for 'spread' firing.

His secondary pulse weapons rapid-fire charged (10 megawatt) energy particles, creating a distinctive 'firewall' effect.

VEHICLE MODE

- On Earth, Optimus Prime transforms into a deluxe six-wheel drive Semi-truck, with an 850 HP engine and a maximum speed of 250mph.
- Vehicular mode is equipped with 39 independent artillery muzzles and roof-mounted surface-to-air missiles.
- A special 'slow-burn' engine continually recycles expended fuel, adding miles to his range.

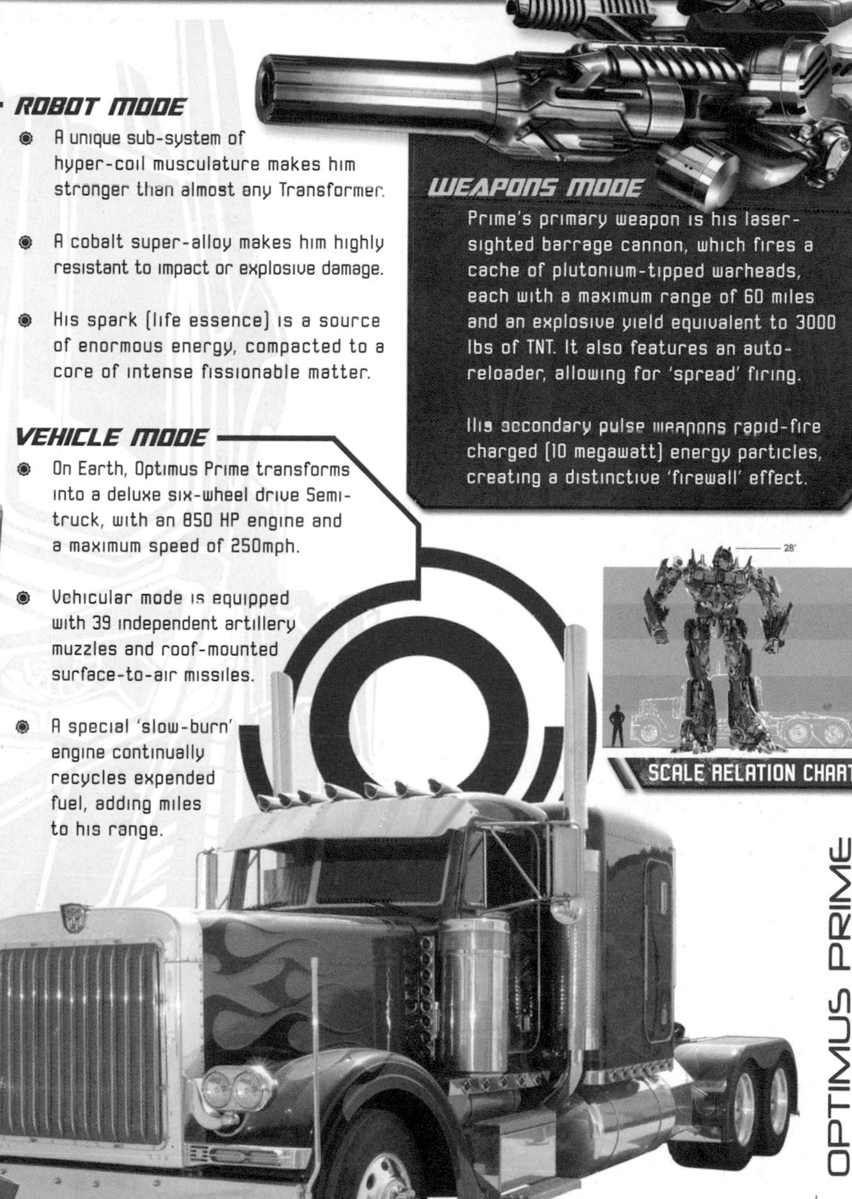

CYBERTRON:
SUDDENLY IT ALL MAKES SENSE. THE DIVERSIONS, THE DISTRACTIONS, THE FALSE TRAILS.
MEGATRON
OPTIMUS PRIME'S INTENTION WAS TO KEEP ME FROM THE ALLSPARK JUST LONG ENOUGH TO LOSE IT IN THE VASTNESS OF THE COSMOS.
I'M SO VERY NEARLY IMPRESSED.

SCRIPT SIMON FURMAN • ART NICK ROCHE • COLOU LAIM SHALLOO • LETTERS BETANCOURT/COMICRAFT

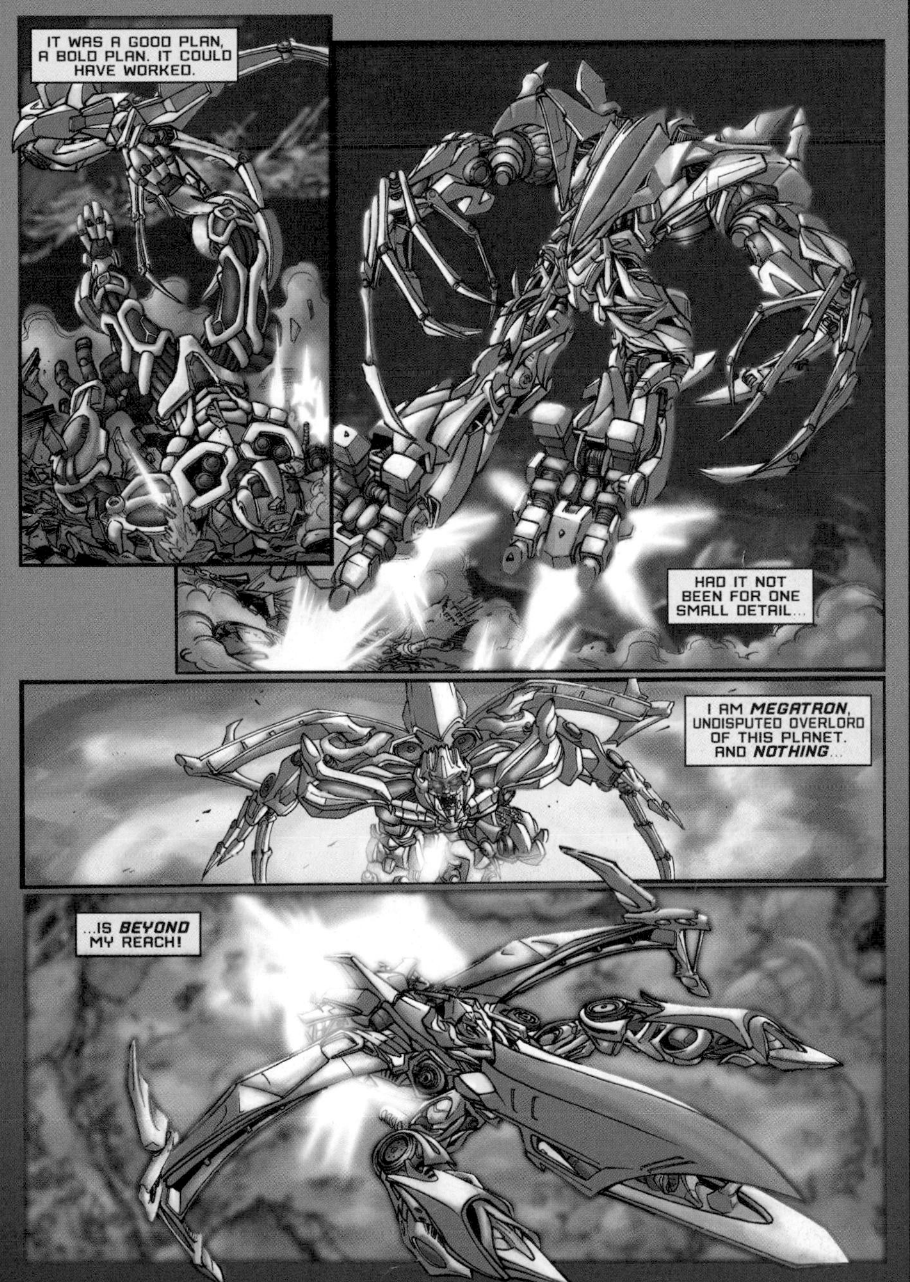
IT WAS A GOOD PLAN, A BOLD PLAN. IT COULD HAVE WORKED.
HAD IT NOT BEEN FOR ONE SMALL DETAIL...
I AM *MEGATRON*, UNDISPUTED OVERLORD OF THIS PLANET. AND *NOTHING*...
...IS *BEYOND* MY REACH!

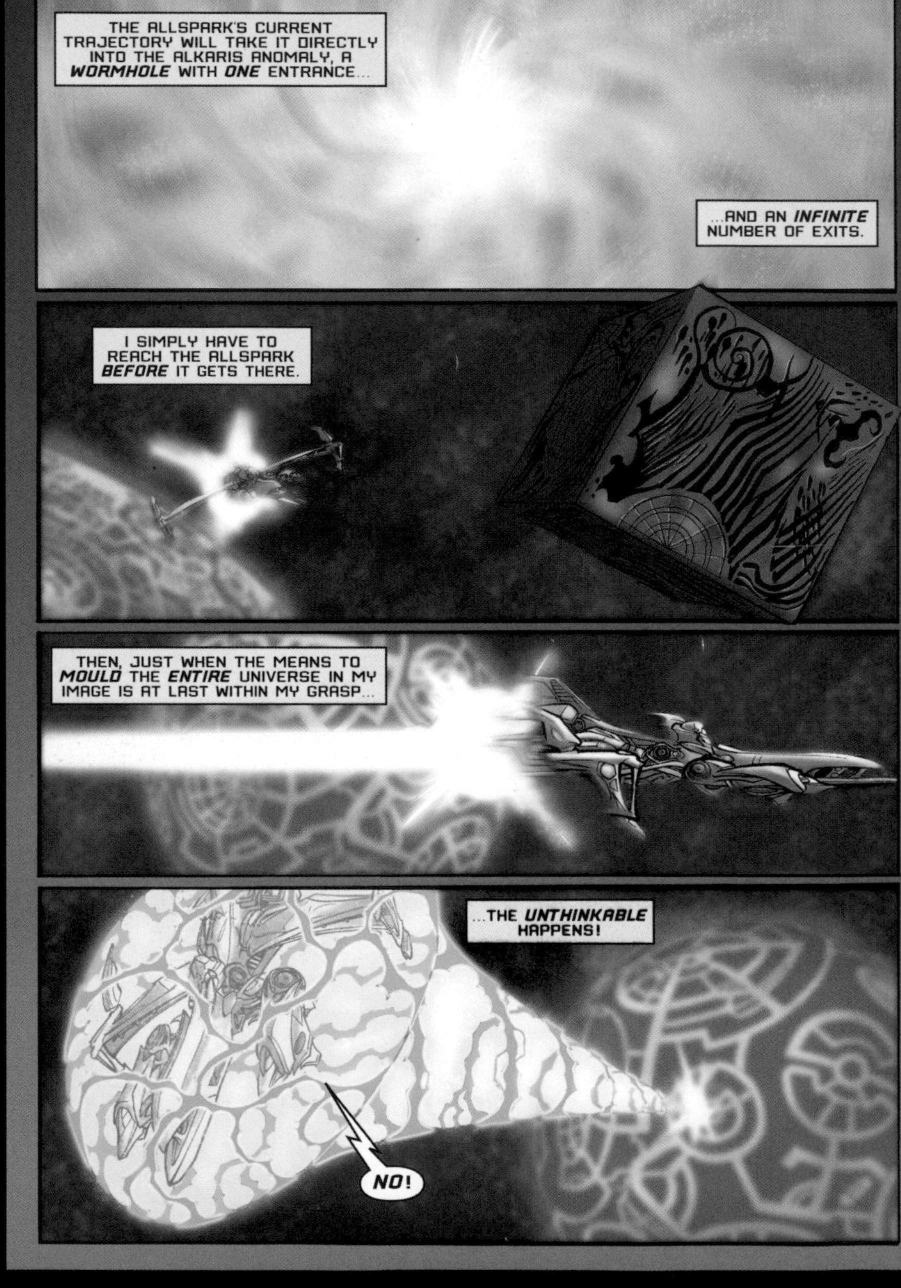
THE ALLSPARK'S CURRENT TRAJECTORY WILL TAKE IT DIRECTLY INTO THE ALKARIS ANOMALY, A *WORMHOLE* WITH *ONE* ENTRANCE...
...AND AN *INFINITE* NUMBER OF EXITS.
I SIMPLY HAVE TO REACH THE ALLSPARK *BEFORE* IT GETS THERE.
THEN, JUST WHEN THE MEANS TO *MOULD* THE *ENTIRE* UNIVERSE IN MY IMAGE IS AT LAST WITHIN MY GRASP...
...THE *UNTHINKABLE* HAPPENS!
NO!

A TRACTOR BEAM... OF SUFFICIENT COHESIVE DENSITY TO CONTAIN EVEN ME!
I LET THEM REEL ME IN...
AND THEN, WHEN I'M WITHIN RANGE...
THRRUMPH
...I GENERATE A REVERSE PARTICLE STREAM OF MY OWN!
FREE! AND FOR THIS IGNOMINY...
...SOMEONE MUST PAY!
I FIGURE HE MEANS US, RATCHET.
YOU THINK? OH WELL...
...NEVER DID WANT TO LIVE FOREVER!
BATAW
BATAW

"HERE HE COMES..."
ZRAK
ZRAK
ZRAK
HNOW!
ZA-RAAAKT
HUFF!
FWUSHH
GHT!
THE URGE TO ENGAGE MY GROUND COMBAT MODE AND *SCRAP* THESE FOOLHARDY AUTOBOTS WITH MY BARE HANDS IS ALMOST OVERWHELMING.
BUT *THAT*...

...IS EXACTLY WHAT PRIME WANTS.
EVERY NANO-KLIK I WASTE ON ENDING THEIR PITIFUL LIVES THE CLOSER THE ALLSPARK COMES TO THE WORMHOLE THRESHOLD. SO, INSTEAD...
...I DELEGATE.
FOR DARING TO ENGAGE ME DIRECTLY...
FDAMMM

...I GIVE THEM...
...DEVASTATOR!
AHEAD, THE ALLSPARK ENTERS THE WORMHOLE'S EVENT HORIZON.
I HAVE MOMENTS TO ACT.

WHATEVER HAPPENS, I'LL NEVER GIVE UP –

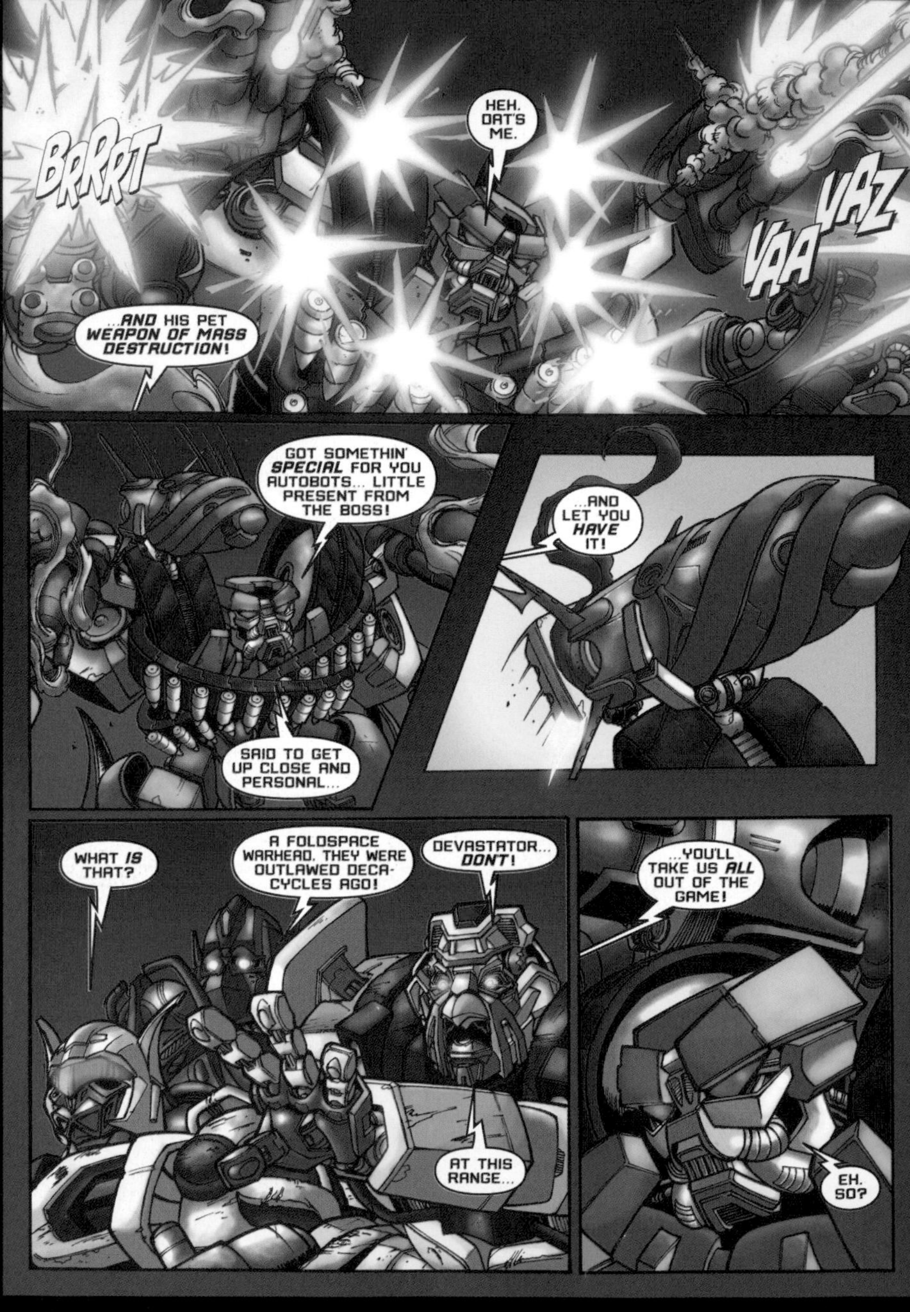
BRRRT
HEH. DAT'S ME.
VAA VAZ
...AND HIS PET WEAPON OF MASS DESTRUCTION!
GOT SOMETHIN' SPECIAL FOR YOU AUTOBOTS... LITTLE PRESENT FROM THE BOSS!
SAID TO GET UP CLOSE AND PERSONAL...
...AND LET YOU HAVE IT!
WHAT IS THAT?
A FOLDSPACE WARHEAD. THEY WERE OUTLAWED DECA-CYCLES AGO!
DEVASTATOR... DON'T!
AT THIS RANGE...
...YOU'LL TAKE US ALL OUT OF THE GAME!
EH. SO?

VOOOSH

VWAAARP

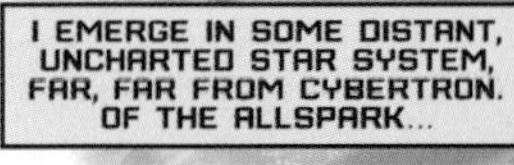
I EMERGE IN SOME DISTANT, UNCHARTED STAR SYSTEM, FAR, FAR FROM CYBERTRON. OF THE ALLSPARK...
...THERE IS ***NO TRACE***.

IT, LIKE THE AUTOBOTS WHO SO CRITICALLY WAYLAID ME...

...IS ***LOST*** IN SPACE.

MEGATRON

INTRODUCTION

No one knows when Megatron changed from the firm but even-handed Lord High Protector of Cybertron into the megalomaniacal tyrant who ignited a devastating civil war. Perhaps the seeds of that brutal warmonger were there all along, hidden behind a mask of compliance, or perhaps The Allspark inadvertently ignited some ancient evil at Megatron's core. Either way, now Megatron will stop at nothing to possess the Allspark, even if Cybertron is destroyed in the process. This utterly single-minded goal makes him a threat of epic proportions, because there is simply no reasoning with him.

HISTORY

It was Megatron who first dared to dream of unlocking the buried potential in the Cybertronian race. Already possessing the power to trans-scan a vehicle or other form and reformat their body accordingly, Megatron believed that the Allspark would give them the capacity to simply *imagine* another form and make it instant reality. So it was that he attempted a direct interface with The Allspark, an act forbidden under Cybertronian law. The pain was terrible, but when he recovered, Megatron tested his new ability by imagining an interstellar jet mode of awesome power and lethality. Thus armed, he began his plans for conquest in earnest.

WEAPONS MODE

Megatron possesses a wide variety of in-built weapons, including barrage cannons that fire lethal fragmentation shells, but he largely prefers to crush or eviscerate his enemies with his bare hands, which are tipped with razor-sharp, diamond-hard claws.

ROBOT MODE

- Megatron's power core is fuelled by unstable dark matter, making him almost unstoppable.
- Any damage Megatron sustains is self-repaired almost immediately.
- His optics double as energy conduits, channelling bursts of super-heated plasma energy.

SCALE RELATION CHART

VEHICLE MODE

- Megatron's jet mode is virtually soundless in flight, with a wide array of dedicated stealth features.
- The vessel's carbon derivative hull absorbs solar and cosmic energy while in flight, and acts as a heat shield when entering a planetary atmosphere.
- Armed with forward barrage weapons and wing-tip lightning generators, the jet also possesses a matter-inversion [tractor] beam.

SCRIPT SIMON FURMAN • **ART** ANDREW WILDMAN/WILD-IDEAS • **LETTERS** JIMMY BETANCOURT/COMICRAFT

I REALLY DON'T WANT TO GET INVOLVED IN OFFWORLD DISPUTES. BUT...
THRRT
... THIS LOT ARE MAKING IT *DIFFICULT* TO STAY NEUTRAL.
PTM
PTM
SO...
... *I CUT UP ROUGH!*
ZREEEK

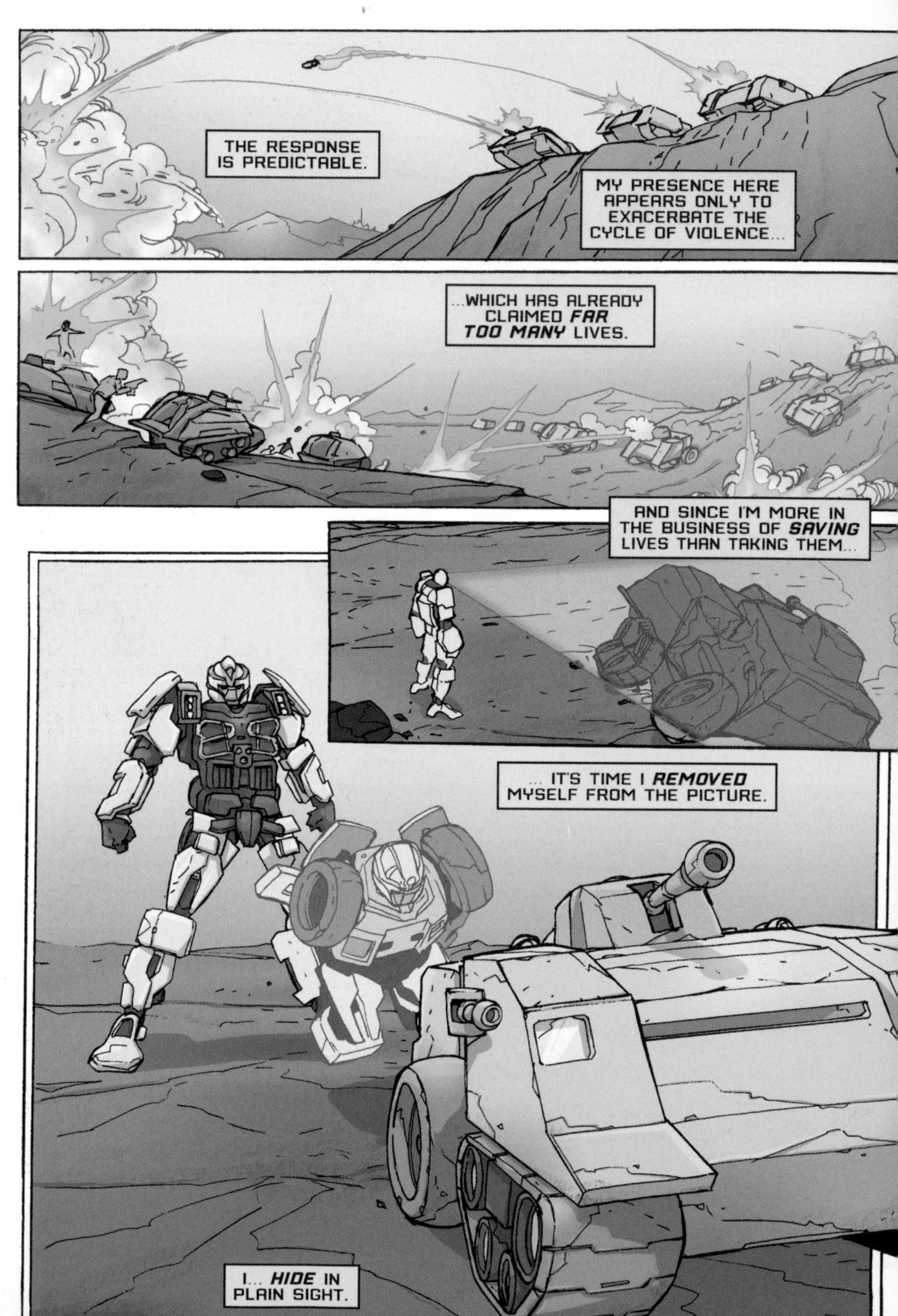
THE RESPONSE IS PREDICTABLE.
MY PRESENCE HERE APPEARS ONLY TO EXACERBATE THE CYCLE OF VIOLENCE...
...WHICH HAS ALREADY CLAIMED FAR TOO MANY LIVES.
AND SINCE I'M MORE IN THE BUSINESS OF SAVING LIVES THAN TAKING THEM...
... IT'S TIME I REMOVED MYSELF FROM THE PICTURE.
I... HIDE IN PLAIN SIGHT.

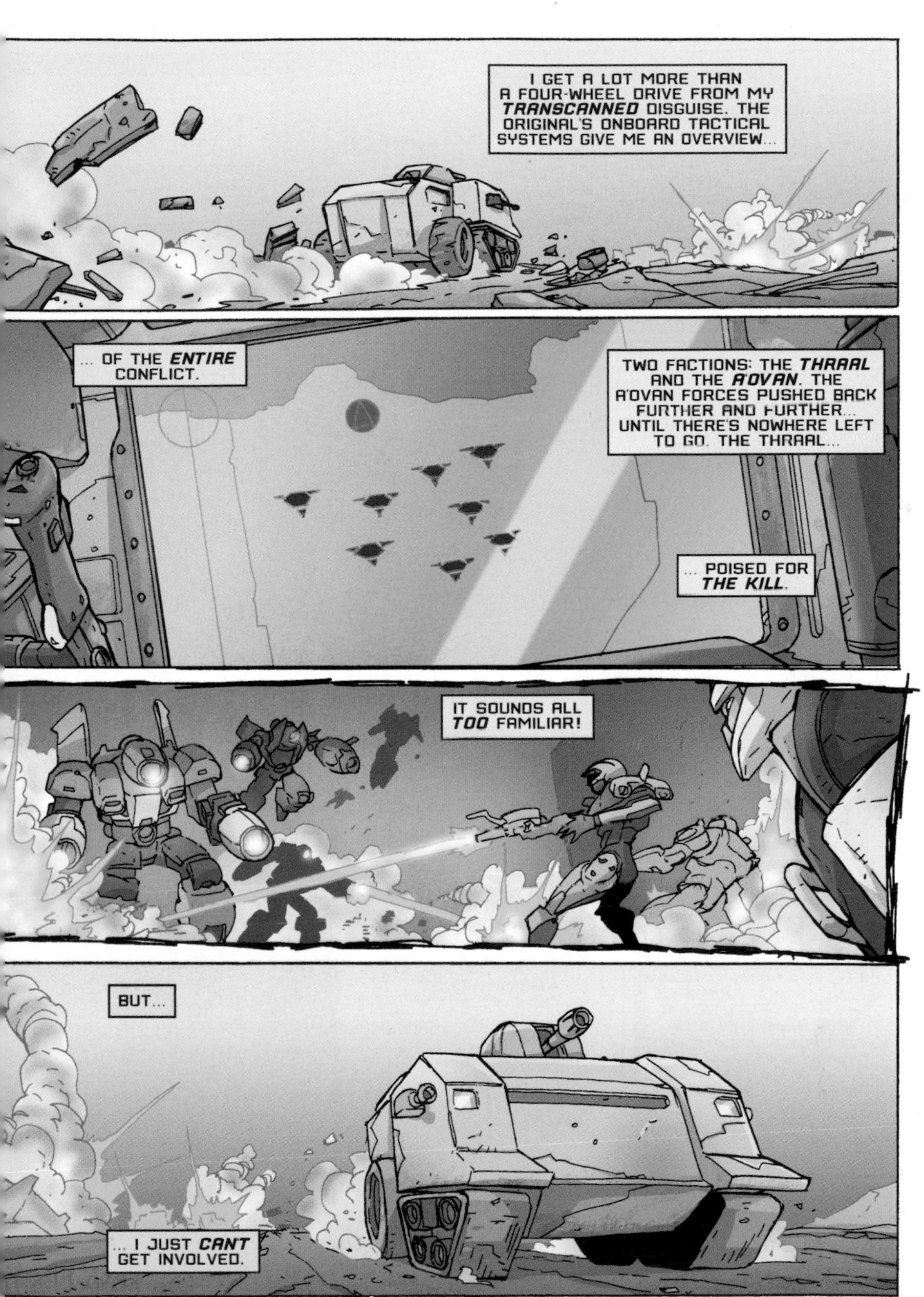
I GET A LOT MORE THAN A FOUR-WHEEL DRIVE FROM MY TRANSCANNED DISGUISE. THE ORIGINAL'S ONBOARD TACTICAL SYSTEMS GIVE ME AN OVERVIEW...
... OF THE ENTIRE CONFLICT.
TWO FACTIONS: THE THRAAL AND THE A'OVAN. THE A'OVAN FORCES PUSHED BACK FURTHER AND FURTHER... UNTIL THERE'S NOWHERE LEFT TO GO. THE THRAAL...
... POISED FOR THE KILL.
IT SOUNDS ALL TOO FAMILIAR!
BUT...
... I JUST CAN'T GET INVOLVED.

RIGHT NOW, MY OWN WORLD IS TEETERING ON THE BRINK OF EXTINCTION. THOUGH WE MANAGED TO DELAY **MEGATRON**...
... HE STILL HAS THE **ALLSPARK** IN HIS SIGHTS.
I **HAVE** TO FIND THE OTHERS.

WHICH REQUIRES A LEVEL-SEVEN SIGNAL BEACON...

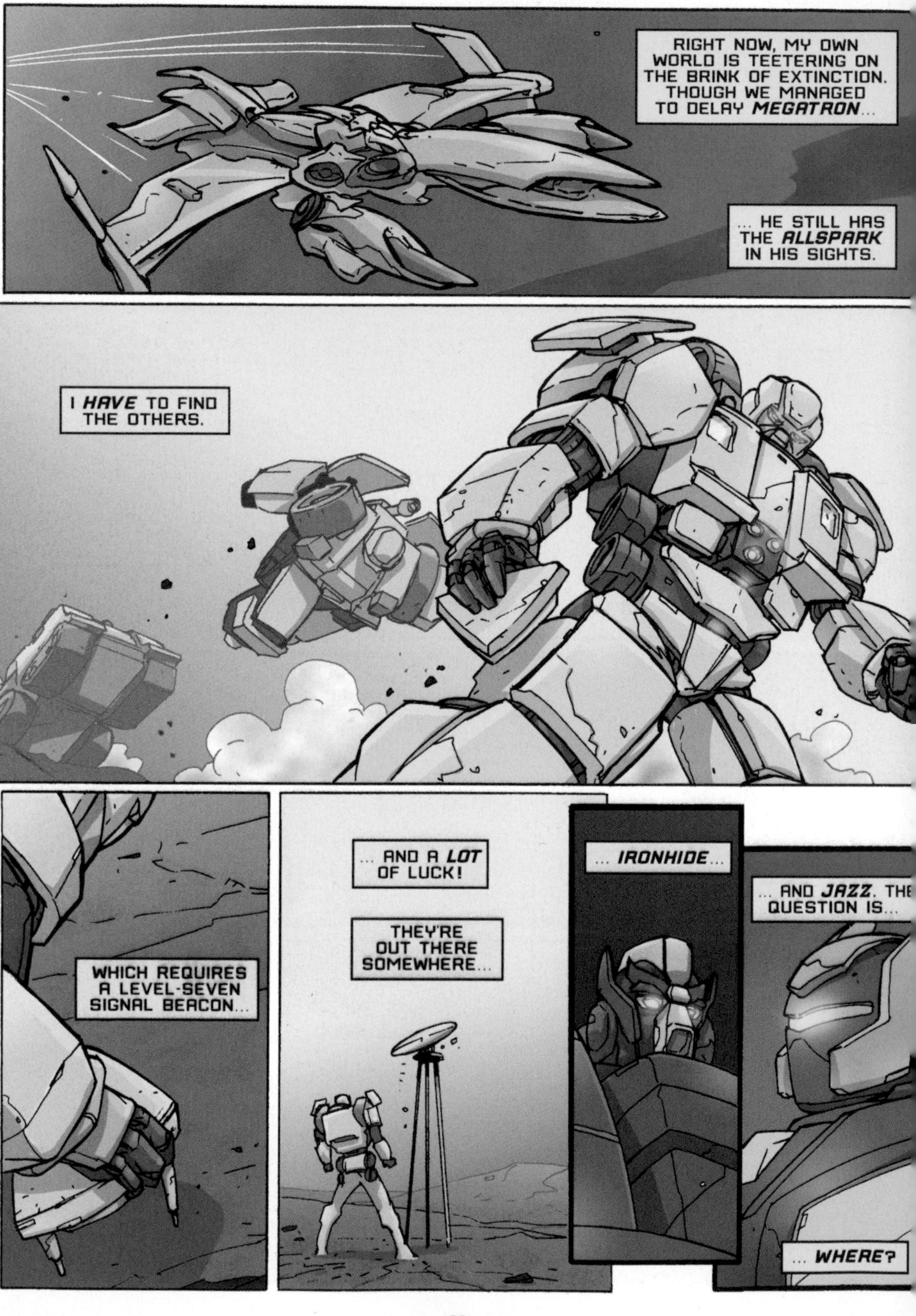

... AND A **LOT** OF LUCK!
THEY'RE OUT THERE SOMEWHERE...
... **IRONHIDE**...
... AND **JAZZ**. THE QUESTION IS...
... **WHERE?**

NOTHING TO DO NOW...
... BUT WAIT.
OR IS THERE?
R'OVAN FORCES...
... SURRENDER OR DIE.
DURGUTH, OF THE THRAAL, HAS SPOKEN!

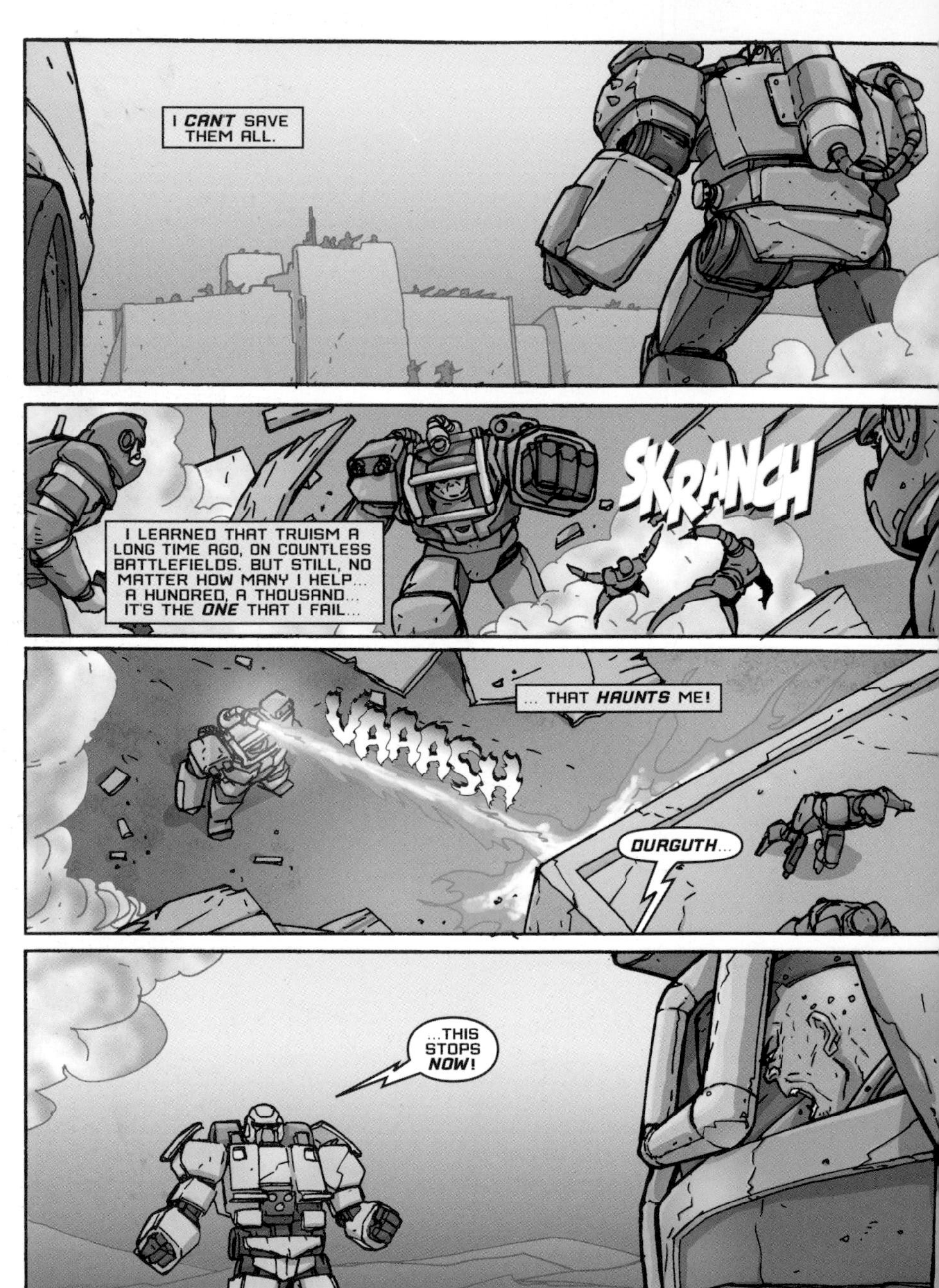
I CAN'T SAVE THEM ALL.
I LEARNED THAT TRUISM A LONG TIME AGO, ON COUNTLESS BATTLEFIELDS. BUT STILL, NO MATTER HOW MANY I HELP... A HUNDRED, A THOUSAND... IT'S THE ONE THAT I FAIL...
SKRANCH
... THAT HAUNTS ME!
VAAASH
DURGUTH...
...THIS STOPS NOW!

I DON'T *EXPECT* HIM TO CAPITULATE.
VA-RAK VA-RAK
HIS TYPE *NEVER* DO!
YOU MAY BE THE TOKEN TYRANT HEREABOUTS, DURGUTH, BUT TRUST ME, ON A *COSMIC* SCALE...
... YOU DON'T EVEN RATE!
ZROT

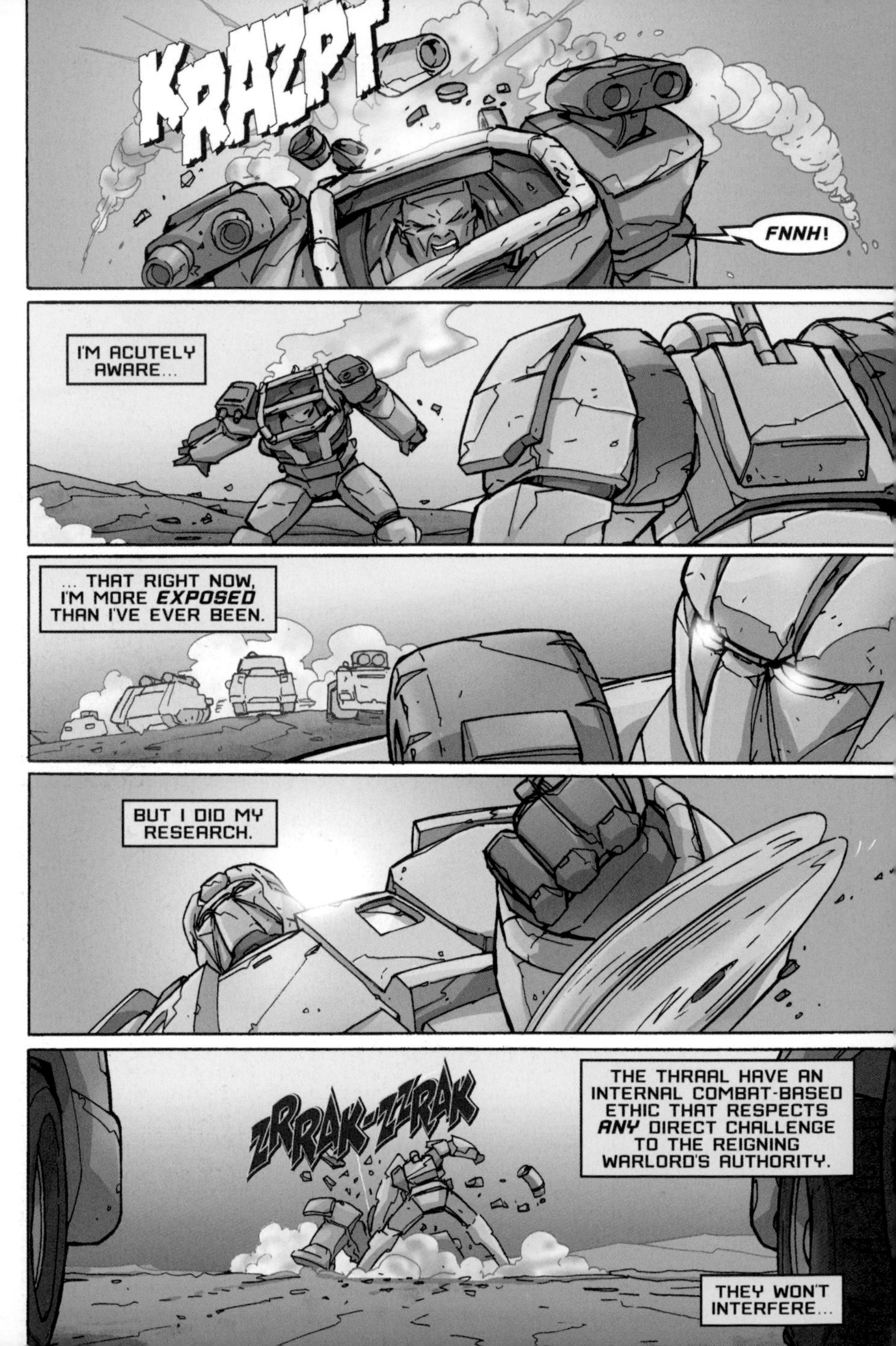
KRAZPT
FNNH!
I'M ACUTELY AWARE...
... THAT RIGHT NOW, I'M MORE EXPOSED THAN I'VE EVER BEEN.
BUT I DID MY RESEARCH.
ZRRAK-ZZRAK
THE THRAAL HAVE AN INTERNAL COMBAT-BASED ETHIC THAT RESPECTS ANY DIRECT CHALLENGE TO THE REIGNING WARLORD'S AUTHORITY.
THEY WON'T INTERFERE...

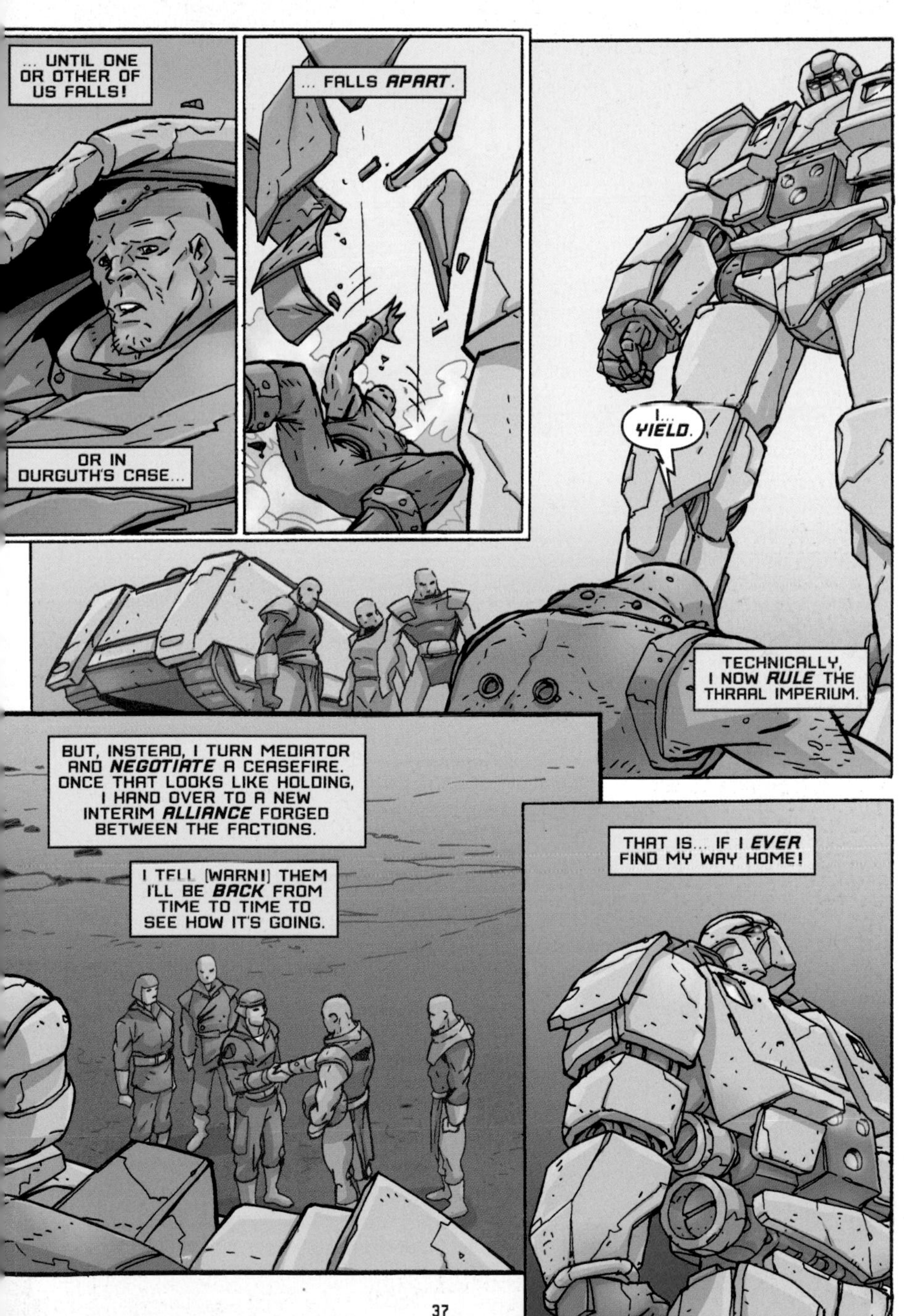
... UNTIL ONE OR OTHER OF US FALLS!
OR IN DURGUTH'S CASE...
... FALLS APART.
I... YIELD.
TECHNICALLY, I NOW RULE THE THRAAL IMPERIUM.
BUT, INSTEAD, I TURN MEDIATOR AND NEGOTIATE A CEASEFIRE. ONCE THAT LOOKS LIKE HOLDING, I HAND OVER TO A NEW INTERIM ALLIANCE FORGED BETWEEN THE FACTIONS.
I TELL [WARN!] THEM I'LL BE BACK FROM TIME TO TIME TO SEE HOW IT'S GOING.
THAT IS... IF I EVER FIND MY WAY HOME!

AUTOBOT VS DECEPTICON SMACKDOWN!

MEGATRON V OPTIMUS PRIME

COMMENTATOR: SIMON FURMAN

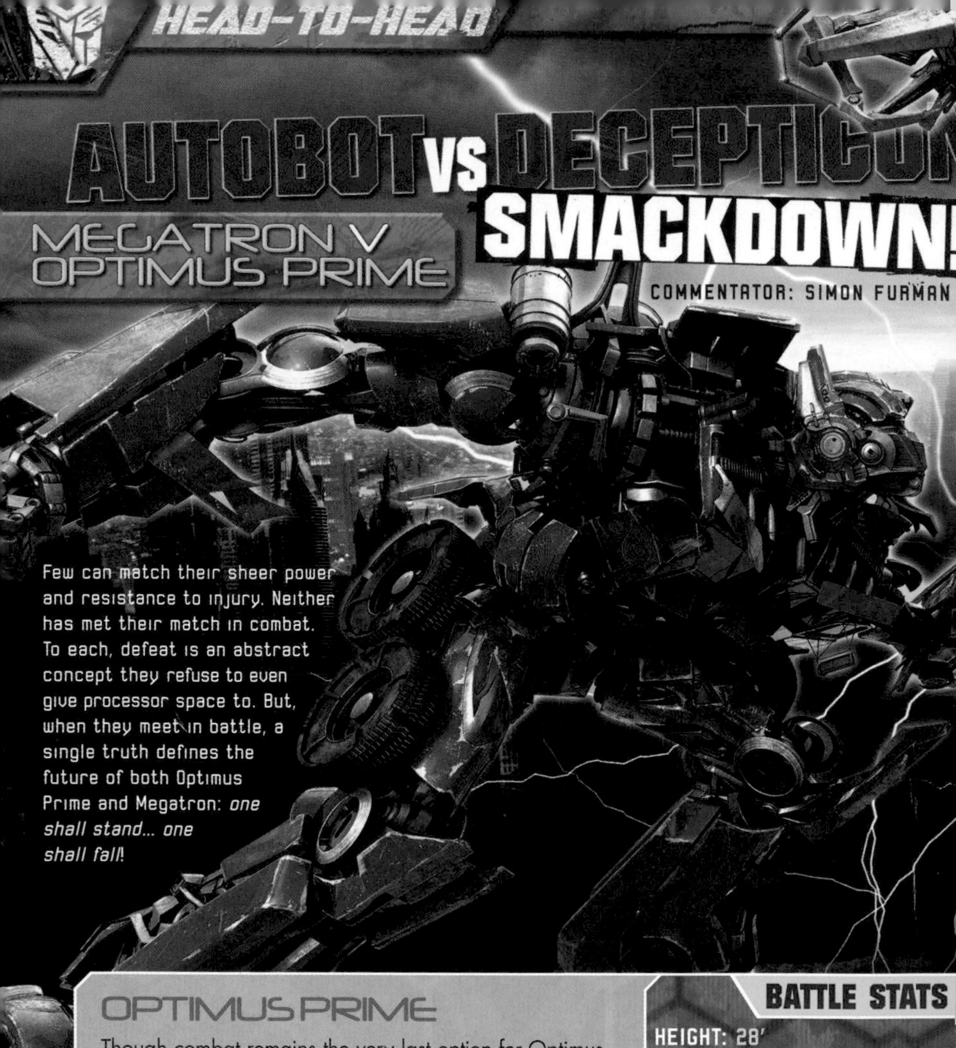

Few can match their sheer power and resistance to injury. Neither has met their match in combat. To each, defeat is an abstract concept they refuse to even give processor space to. But, when they meet in battle, a single truth defines the future of both Optimus Prime and Megatron: *one shall stand... one shall fall!*

OPTIMUS PRIME

Though combat remains the very last option for Optimus Prime, he is remarkably efficient at it, even proficient. When Prime first reluctantly took up arms in the wake of Megatron's declaration of war, he immersed himself in the whole sweeping history of intergalactic warfare, studying whole campaigns, personal odysseys and every desperate last stand, becoming a master strategist. Prime understands that in the heat of battle, compassion is a luxury he simply cannot afford.

BATTLE STATS

HEIGHT: 28'

WEIGHT: 4.3 TONNES

MAX. SPEED: 250 MPH

POWER LEVEL:

ENDURANCE:

SKILL:

FUUSHH
I NEED TO LET OFF STEAM...

BADDAADOOM
...VENT SOME FRUSTRATION...

...AND JUST DO WHAT I DO BEST.
KRREENT

WHICH IS TAKE THINGS APART... WHOLESALE.
THRMKKK

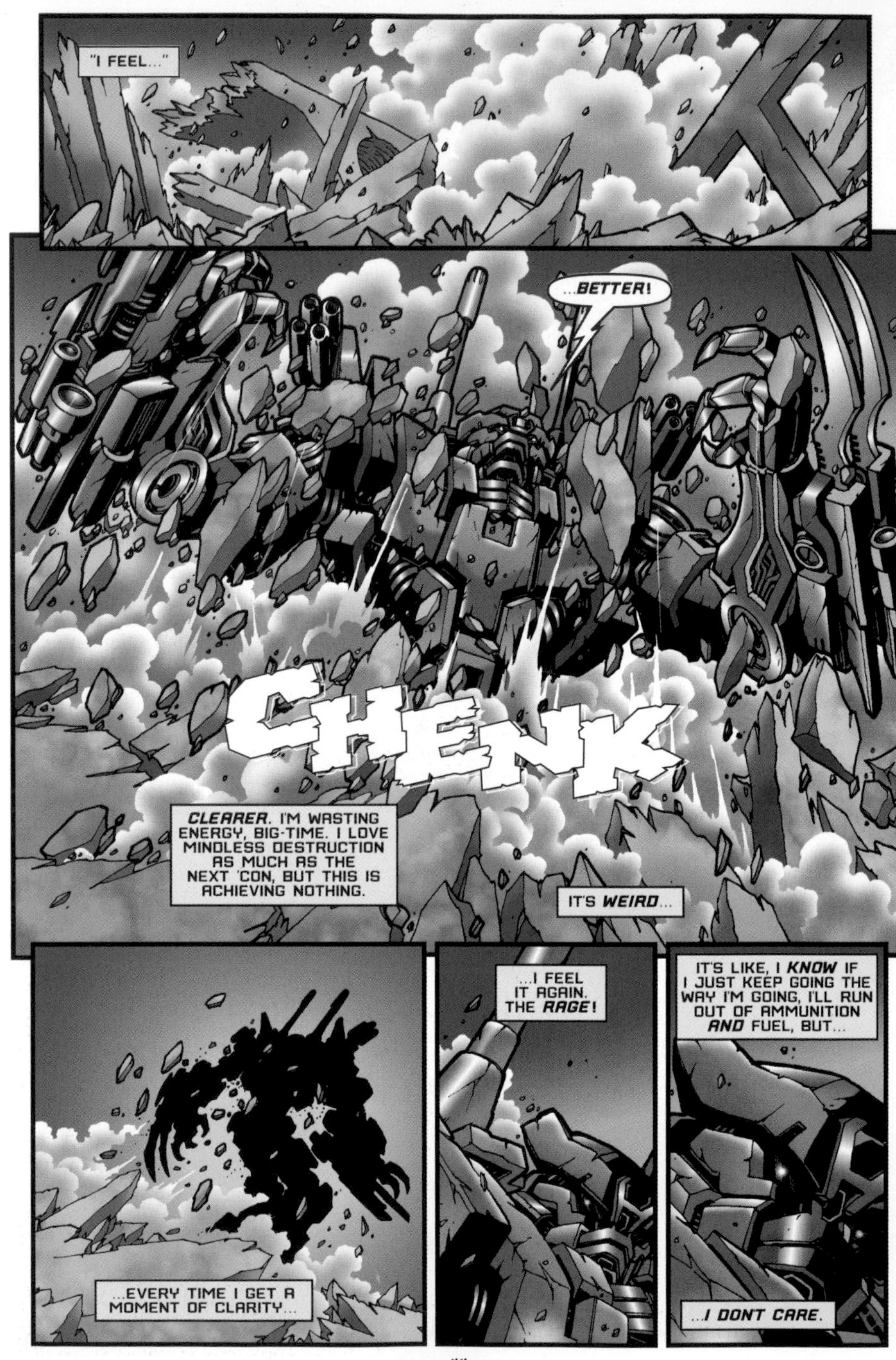
"I FEEL..."
...BETTER!
CHENK
CLEARER. I'M WASTING ENERGY, BIG-TIME. I LOVE MINDLESS DESTRUCTION AS MUCH AS THE NEXT 'CON, BUT THIS IS ACHIEVING NOTHING.
IT'S WEIRD...
...EVERY TIME I GET A MOMENT OF CLARITY...
...I FEEL IT AGAIN. THE RAGE!
IT'S LIKE, I KNOW IF I JUST KEEP GOING THE WAY I'M GOING, I'LL RUN OUT OF AMMUNITION AND FUEL, BUT...
...I DONT CARE.

I HAVE TO STOP, FIGURE OUT A WAY OFF THIS PLANET. BUT I...
...CANT!
SKRRRRAM
GOTTA GET A GRIP!
NEED TO JUICE UP, RE-CHARGE MY INTER-PLANETARY THRUSTERS.
AND GO FIND MYSELF SOME AUTOBOTS TO MANGLE.
BUT FIRST...

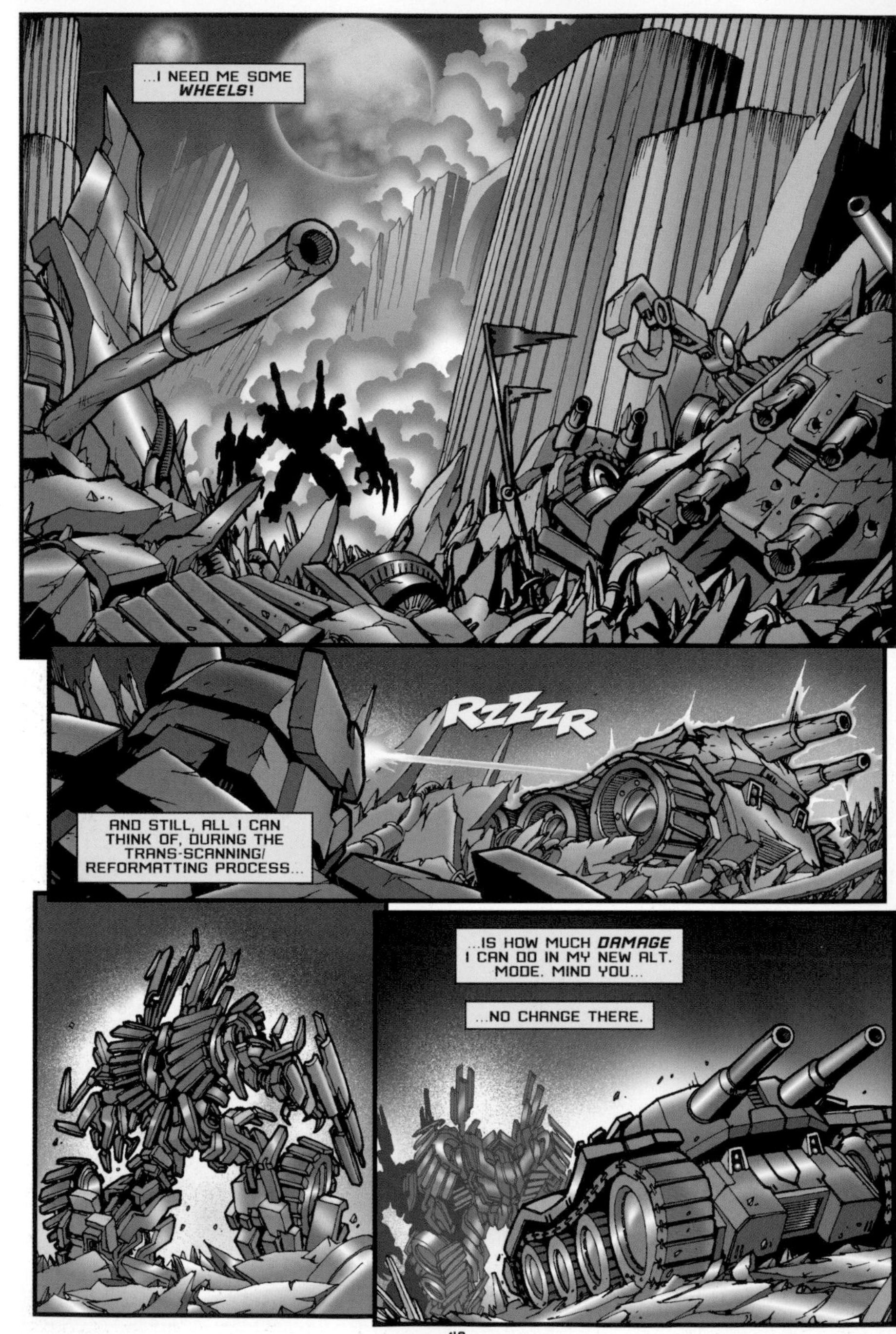
...I NEED ME SOME WHEELS!
RZZZR
AND STILL, ALL I CAN THINK OF, DURING THE TRANS-SCANNING/ REFORMATTING PROCESS...
...IS HOW MUCH DAMAGE I CAN DO IN MY NEW ALT. MODE. MIND YOU...
...NO CHANGE THERE.

I FINALLY LOCK ONTO AN ENERGY SOURCE AND HOME IN ON IT.
THE CLOSER I GET, THE STRONGER THE FEELING...
...I'M NOT ALONE.
STOP! GO NO FURTHER! IF YOU VALUE WHAT'S LEFT OF YOUR SANITY...
...TURN AROUND NOW!
THE FLAME WILL CONSUME YOU, UTTERLY, AS IT DID US. WE WERE A PEACEFUL RACE, UN-VERSED IN THE WAYS OF WAR, UNTIL THE FLAME...
WHATEVER.
...BECAME A CONFLAGRATION, FANNING OUR OWN WORST INSTINCTS. WE TURNED ON EACH OTHER...
...AND MADE THIS WORLD A WASTELAND.

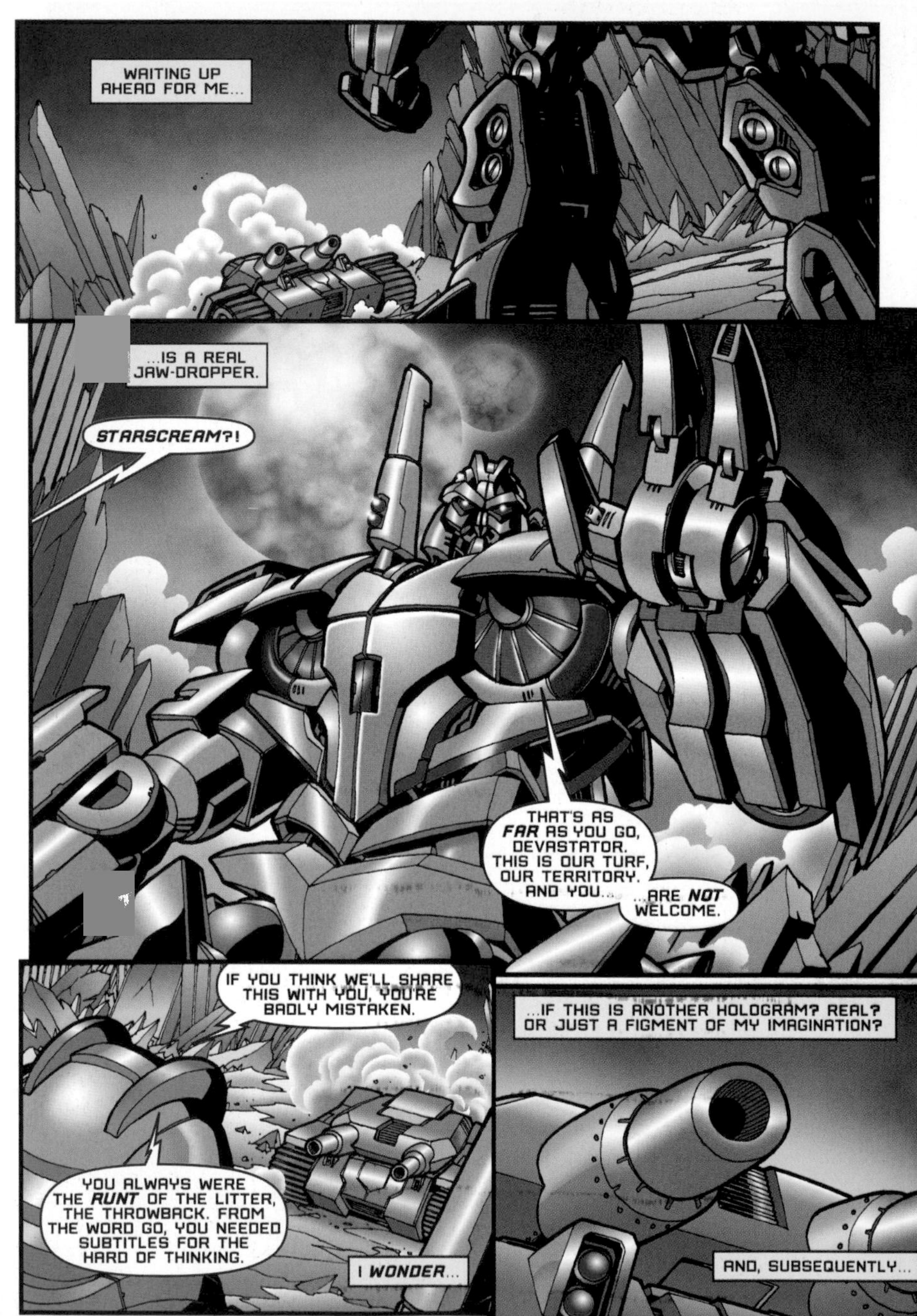
WAITING UP AHEAD FOR ME...
...IS A REAL JAW-DROPPER.
STARSCREAM?!
THAT'S AS FAR AS YOU GO, DEVASTATOR. THIS IS OUR TURF, OUR TERRITORY. AND YOU...
...ARE NOT WELCOME.
IF YOU THINK WE'LL SHARE THIS WITH YOU, YOU'RE BADLY MISTAKEN.
YOU ALWAYS WERE THE RUNT OF THE LITTER, THE THROWBACK. FROM THE WORD GO, YOU NEEDED SUBTITLES FOR THE HARD OF THINKING.
I WONDER...
...IF THIS IS ANOTHER HOLOGRAM? REAL? OR JUST A FIGMENT OF MY IMAGINATION?
AND, SUBSEQUENTLY...

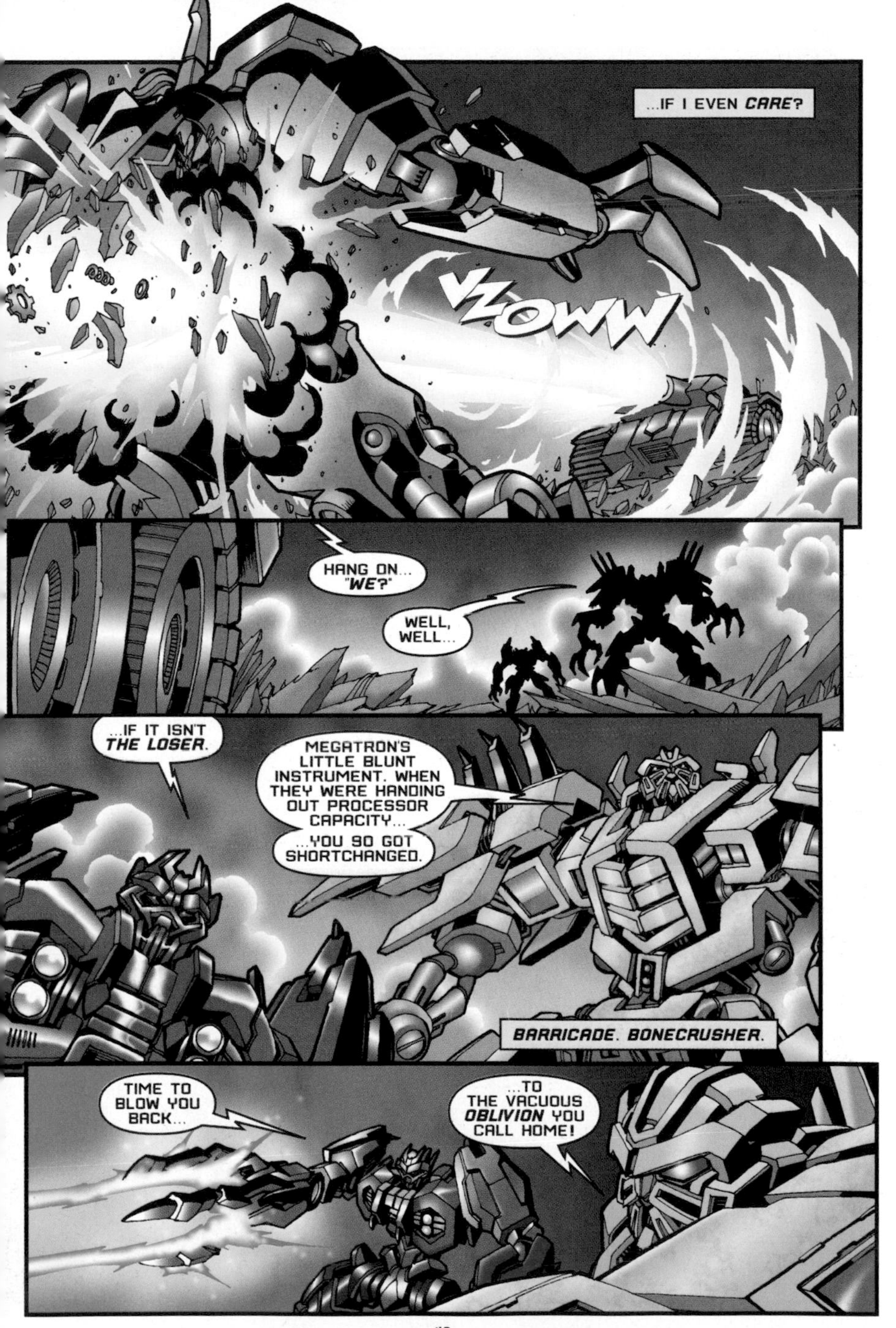
...IF I EVEN CARE?
VZOWW
HANG ON... "WE?"
WELL, WELL...
...IF IT ISN'T THE LOSER.
MEGATRON'S LITTLE BLUNT INSTRUMENT. WHEN THEY WERE HANDING OUT PROCESSOR CAPACITY...
...YOU SO GOT SHORTCHANGED.
BARRICADE. BONECRUSHER.
TIME TO BLOW YOU BACK...
...TO THE VACUOUS OBLIVION YOU CALL HOME!

FN-UNHH!
TKOW
VAAP
FEELS REAL ENOUGH.
BUT IF THEY THINK THEIR WEAPONS--OR THEIR WORDS--CAN HURT ME...
BAKOW
...THEY REALLY DON'T KNOW ME AT ALL!
SEE, ME, I GO BY ONE GUIDING PRINCIPLE — KEEP IT STUPID...
BAKOW
...SIMPLE!

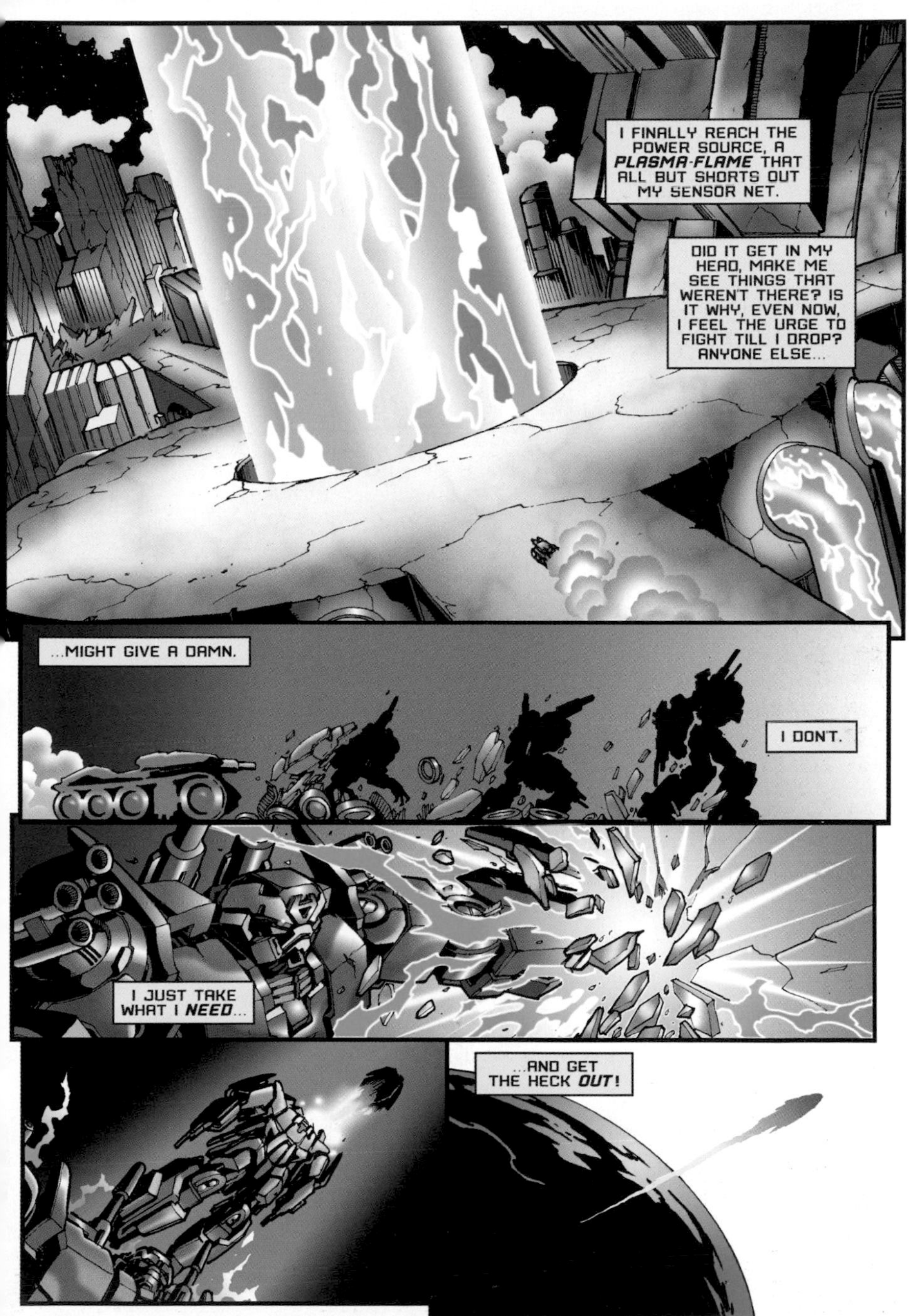
I FINALLY REACH THE POWER SOURCE, A *PLASMA-FLAME* THAT ALL BUT SHORTS OUT MY SENSOR NET.
DID IT GET IN MY HEAD, MAKE ME SEE THINGS THAT WEREN'T THERE? IS IT WHY, EVEN NOW, I FEEL THE URGE TO FIGHT TILL I DROP? ANYONE ELSE...
...MIGHT GIVE A DAMN.
I DON'T.
I JUST TAKE WHAT I *NEED*...
...AND GET THE HECK *OUT*!

JAZZ

INTRODUCTION

One of the most adaptable and inquisitive of all the Autobots, Jazz absorbs facts and figures like a sponge. On arrival on any given alien world, Jazz taps right into the local information highways, quickly assimilates the details of his environment and relays them (in distilled fashion) to his fellow Autobots. On any kind of exploration or infiltration mission outside of Cybertronian space, he's nigh-on essential to its success. He's also a naturally cool customer, even under intense fire.

HISTORY

SCRATCH THE SURFACE

Jazz is very adroit and on the ball when it comes to making things happen. He can get you exactly what you need for the job at hand, even when you're far from home and what you need is seemingly nowhere at hand. But while Jazz is most at home away from home, he also proved himself an essential part of the war effort on Cybertron. Able to process raw battlefield data at an amazing speed and output focused tactical info-feeds, Jazz could make or break an engagement with the Decepticons. Ultimately, Optimus Prime recognised Jazz's unique contribution by promoting him to First Lieutenant, an appointment that raised one or two optical shields. Jazz's thinly-veiled vanity and reluctance to engage in combat in vehicular mode (for fear of picking up a dent or scratch) hasn't always sat well with his fellow Autobots.

WEAPONS MODE

- Built to Jazz's own rigorous designs, his tritanium composite battle shield has an integrated cryo-emitter.
- Laced with tactical sensors that can 'predict' an attack, the shield is highly durable and the cryo-emitter can freeze an opponent in a matter of seconds.
- The shield can also project heat; the mix of cold and heat can crack the toughest armour.

ROBOT MODE

- Jazz's armour has a friction-retardant surface, meaning that even on two feet he's very fast.
- His analytical visor and [body-wide] sensor net help him predict and assess atmospheric and environmental conditions.
- The visor can access a wide variety of vision options, including X-Ray, thermal, infrared and microscopic.

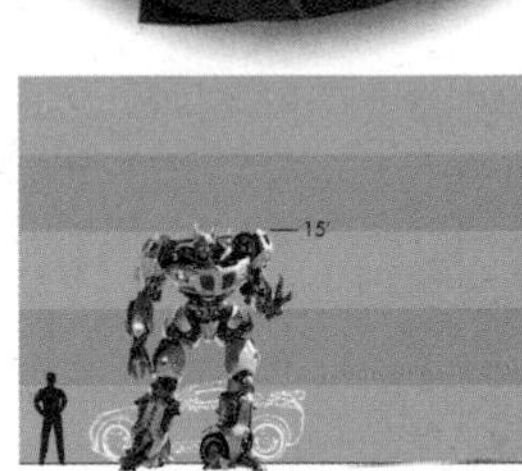

SCALE RELATION CHART

VEHICLE MODE

- Jazz invariably selects something sporty, pricey and guaranteed to turn heads for his vehicle mode.
- His current Earth mode is a silver Pontiac Solstice. Jazz clearly knows the difference between what's functional... and what's cool!
- His vehicular mode has a cryo-emitter weapon, which fires jets of freezing liquid nitrogen, and unique acceleration features.

JAZZ

IRON HIDE
AFTER SEVERAL SOLAR CYCLES' WORTH OF PLANET-HOPPING, I FINALLY PICK UP A HOMING SIGNAL FROM RATCHET* AND SET COURSE.
EN ROUTE...
...I'M *CAUGHT*.
WHOEVER THEY ARE, THEY DON'T KNOW *WHAT* THEY'VE LET THEMSELVES IN FOR!
LOST IN SPACE
PART 3

SCRIPT SIMON FURMAN • **ARTWORK** GUIDO GUIDI • **COLOURS** JASON CARDY • **LETTERING** JIMMY BETANCOURT/COMICRAFT

...*LATER*.

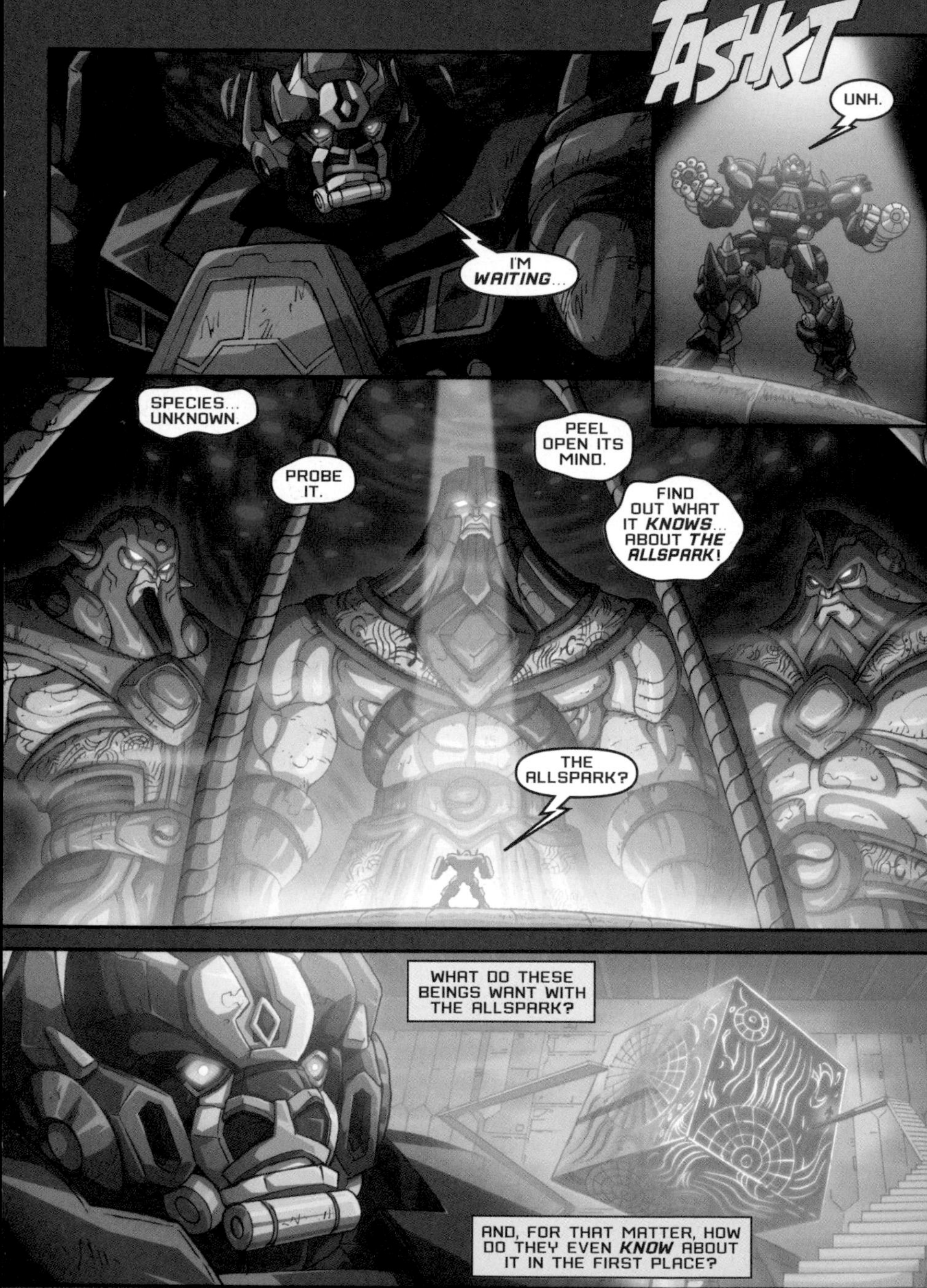
I'M WAITING...
TASHKT
UNH.
SPECIES... UNKNOWN.
PROBE IT.
PEEL OPEN ITS MIND.
FIND OUT WHAT IT KNOWS... ABOUT THE ALLSPARK!
THE ALLSPARK?
WHAT DO THESE BEINGS WANT WITH THE ALLSPARK?
AND, FOR THAT MATTER, HOW DO THEY EVEN KNOW ABOUT IT IN THE FIRST PLACE?

THE ALLSPARK IS OURS. IT WAS STOLEN, MANY MILLENNIA AGO.
YOU HAVE ITS MARK UPON YOU.
YOU...

...WILL TELL US. EVERYTHING.
FN-UHGH.
IN-INSIDE MY HEAD!
I KNOW A LITTLE ABOUT INTERROGATION TECHNIQUES. AND HOW TO RESIST!
THE REST...

...IS SHEER OBSTINACY.
YOU HEARD ME...
...CHARAARGE!

WE LEAVE NO ONE BEHIND. THAT'S THE FIRST RULE OF SOLDIERING.
WHAT'S THE SECOND?
LEAVE NO ONE BEHIND.
RIGHT!
BUT... THIS IS SUICIDE!
THERE MUST BE WHAT, HALF A DECEPTICON BATTALION HOLED UP IN THERE!
WELL...
FATOOOM
"...GIVE OR TAKE!"

SKYBLAST — LAY DOWN COVERING FIRE.
RIGHT-HO. I MEAN... YESSIR!
SIGNAL FLARE, STRONGARM — FLANKING RUNS. DRAW THE HEAT FROM THOSE GUARD TOWERS.
SOME TRAINING MISSION THIS TURNED OUT TO BE!
IN AT THE DEEP END, EH?
BUMPER, SLIPSTREAM... YOU'RE WITH ME.
STAY CLOSE.
F-TUM
F-TUM
ZZRAKZ
"YOU'RE AT THE SHARP END NOW!"

PTOW
PTOW
IRONHIDE — LOOK!
THE GUARD TOWERS, THEY'RE —
AUTOMATED. I KNOW.

IT'S... DESERTED.
MOST OF THEM ARE. MEGATRON'S FORCES ARE SPREAD TOO THIN TO MAN EVERY OUTPOST.
THIRD RULE OF SOLDIERING?
ER... OH!
"TAKE NOTHING AT FACE VALUE."
GOOD ADVICE.
HE'S RESISTING.
BLOCKING OUR PROBES WITH A MEMORY.
I DECIDE TO TAKE IT.
WELL! HAVING CAREFULLY CONSIDERED YOUR VARIOUS PROCLAMATIONS AND CONTENTIONS I FIND THAT THEY ALL...

I *DON'T* KNOCK.

VRANGGG

SURRENDER NOW. OR...

...YOU GOT YOURSELVES A PROBLEM!
CH-CHK

IT TURNS OUT THE CRAFT WAS SALVAGE,

...THE SPOILS INCLUDED HIS — A DEVICE TTUNED TO THE PECIFIC ENERGY TTERNS OF THE LSPARK. INSTEAD OF IT, THEY FOUND ME.
LIKE MEGATRON, THEIR INTENTION WAS TO EXPLOIT THE ALLSPARK. I SEE TO IT THAT THIS IS NO LONGER AN OPTION. BUT, EVEN AS I DEPART, I WONDER WHO ONCE OWNED THIS VESSEL...

...AND WHAT THEIR TRUE CONNECTION TO THE ALLSPARK IS!

AUTOBOT VS DECEPTICON SMACKDOWN!

JAZZ V BLACKOUT

COMMENTATOR: SIMON FURMAN

The Autobots' slick, streamlined alien culture specialist locks horns with the Decepticons' loud, in-your-face shock trooper. Here's how they measure up, their strengths, their weaknesses and their own unique battlefield tactics. Who'd win? You decide...

JAZZ

No one doubts Jazz's courage. He'll go willingly where others fear to tread, simply because it's somewhere he hasn't been before, some brave new world or environment to explore and assess. One of the most adaptable of all Autobots, he absorbs language, culture and geo-political data at a staggering speed, making him vital on any kind of exploration mission. He's adept at processing battlefield data and relaying that information instantly to the forward line.

BATTLE STATS

HEIGHT: 15' 7"

WEIGHT: 1.8 TONNES

MAX. SPEED: 400 MPH

POWER LEVEL:

ENDURANCE:

SKILL:

BATTLE STATS

HEIGHT: 33′ 5″

WEIGHT: 2.9 TONNES

MAX. SPEED: 800 MPH

POWER LEVEL:

ENDURANCE:

SKILL:

BLACKOUT

Something of a coward, Blackout nevertheless revels in the chaos and confusion he sows in his position at the forefront of all major Decepticon attacks. Self-preservation is uppermost in his mind, and the pandemonium he surrounds himself with creates enough of a distraction to ensure few foes ever get a clear shot at him. He strikes from leftfield, descending from on high at great speed, and is quite willing to sacrifice others (fellow Decepticons included) to achieve his goals.

JAZZ

- Jazz is very fast and highly manoeuvrable, his lightweight construction and reduced body mass (he's relatively small compared to other Autobots) making him light on his feet and a blur in vehicular mode.
- His armour plating has a friction-retardant sheen, cutting down wind shear and so increasing his optimum speed.
- Jazz's tactical visor allows him to view the battlefield in a variety of different ways, from thermal to infrared to microscopic. Nothing escapes his attention.

WEAKNESSES

JAZZ'S VANITY IS HIS ACHILLES HEEL. HE'LL OFTEN DIVERT ENERGY FROM HIS VITAL SPARK CORE FORCEFIELD TO PROTECT HIS BODYWORK AND WILL ABANDON HIS VEHICULAR MODE IF THERE'S THE SLIGHTEST POSSIBILITY OF IT SUSTAINING DAMAGE.

BLACKOUT

- Blackout can emit a sonic shriek that both disrupts/overloads electrical systems and disorientates/disables other combatants. The sonic shriek also creates a ripple effect that results in spectacular and combustive pyrotechnics.
- In aerial mode he can fly in virtually all weather conditions and execute a steep attack dive from great height.
- Though not heavily armoured, and vulnerable in aerial mode due to his rotor blades, Blackout can still brawl with the best in robot mode.

WEAKNESSES

BLACKOUT'S SONIC WEAPONRY CAN OCCASIONALLY GENERATE A BACKWASH EFFECT THAT ADVERSELY AFFECTS HIS OWN SYSTEMS. FORCED TO ENGAGE AUDITORY MUFFLERS IN BATTLE, HE CAN BE CAUGHT UNAWARES IF APPROACHED FROM BEHIND.

LOST in SPACE
PART 4
RATCHET'S EMERGENCY SIGNAL BEACON' KEEPS COMING THROUGH AT REGULAR INTERVALS. LOUD AND CLEAR!
I STUDIOUSLY IGNORE IT.
I'M DONE WITH WAR AND STRIFE AND THE PERPETUAL ARMOUR-DENTING GRIND OF LIFE ON CYBERTRON.
EVERYTHING I NEED IS RIGHT HERE!
JAZZ
SCRIPT SIMON FURMAN • ARTWORK MARCELO MATERE
• COLOURS LIAM SHALLOO • LETTERING JIMMY BETANCOURT/COMICRAFT

I'VE DUBBED THIS THE *INFORMATION HIGHWAY*.
THE ACCUMULATED KNOWLEDGE OF COUNTLESS ALIEN CULTURES, CONDENSED INTO A KIND OF SENSORY PRECIPITATION.
I'M IN DATA *OVERDRIVE*, EVERY SUB-SYSTEM EXPLODING WITH CACHES CONTAINING NEW WAYS OF THINKING. OF *BEING*!
SOME DAYS... IT'S ALMOST *TOO* MUCH.

THESE WEREN'T HERE YESTERDAY...
...OR WHENEVER IT WAS I WAS LAST ON THIS LOWER STRATUM...
THE PLANET SEEMS IN A CONSTANT STATE OF *FLUX*, NEVER STILL.
IN THAT RESPECT...
...IT'S A LOT LIKE *ME*!
THAT'S WHAT I LOVE ABOUT THIS PLACE, WHY I JUST DON'T *EVER* WANT TO LEAVE.
THERE'S *ALWAYS* SOMETHING NEW AND WONDERFUL TO EXPERIENCE.
HM.
WHAT'S THE DEAL HERE? I DON'T WANT –

HEY. HEY!
THIS IS DIFFERENT. UP TILL NOW, IT'S ALL BEEN GIVE. WHATEVER THESE THINGS ARE...
...THEY TAKE!
HN-UHHT.
MY PAST...
DID DID WE LOSE HIM?
PROBABLY NOT. WAY I HEAR IT, THERE'S NO HALF MEASURES WITH HIM.
HE NEVER GIVES UP.
UH-HH. CLOCKER — WAIT! I NEED TO REST.
HE ALMOST TORE OUT MY SLAGGIN' SPARK!

I KNOW. IT TOOK EVERYTHING I HAD TO STOP HIM FOLLOWING THROUGH.
WHAT WERE YOU THINKING, EXTERNALIZING YOUR SPARK CORE FORCEFIELD?
HEH. YOU KNOW ME. I LIKE TO KEEP MY BODYWORK BUFF.
KNOW WHAT I LIKE TO DO WITH SHINY THINGS?
OH NO...
...BONECRUSHER!
I LIKE TO TURN THEM INTO SCORCHED, MANGLED WRECKS. 'CAUSE I FIGURE, WHY SHOULD THEY LOOK SO NICE...
...WHEN I LOOK LIKE THIS!

GO!
CONDITION YOU'RE IN, JAZZ, YOU'RE MORE HINDRANCE THAN HELP TO ME.
BUT- I CAN'T-
JUST GO!
VOW!
BY THE TIME I REACHED THE SURFACE AND CALLED IN REINFORCEMENTS, THERE WASN'T MUCH LEFT OF CLOCKER TO SALVAGE.
NOT MY FINEST HOUR.
NEITHER IS THIS.
I RE-ALLOCATED SO MUCH OF MY SYSTEM CAPACITY TO DATA STORAGE THERE'S NOTHING LEFT IN ME TO RESIST.

I CAN FEEL EVERY BIT OF ME BEING SLOWLY STRIPPED AWAY, ABSORBED.
MEMORIES, EXPERIENCES, SENSATIONS...
ALL I CAN DO IS LAUNCH A WARNING BUOY...
FUSH
... AND HOPE OTHERS KEEP AWAY.
TIME PASSES...
I CLING ONTO WHATEVER BRIEF PERIODS OF LUCIDITY I GET, FORMULATING A RATIONALE, A THEORY. I CONCLUDE THAT THE PLANET...
... IS ALIVE!
AND I AM NOT ITS FIRST VICTIM.

JAZZ!
AT FIRST I THINK IT'S MY IMAGINATION OR A RANDOM FRAGMENT OF MY SPLINTERED CONSCIOUSNESS.
SKRRAK
SKRRAK
THEN I REALISE.
THE CAVALRY HAS ARRIVED.
IRONHIDE — THESE THINGS ARE A KIND OF SENSORY APPARATUS, EXTENSIONS OF WHAT AMOUNTS TO A NERVOUS SYSTEM.

YEAH?
SO LET'S GET ITS ATTENTION!
KLKT
BADOOM
ASSUMING YOU CAN HEAR, I'M GOING TO SAY THIS JUST *ONCE*.
GIVE US BACK OUR 'BOT.
THA-WHOOM

STEADY. I'VE GOT YOU.
PTUPP
RR-RATCHET. HOW-?
WE'VE BEEN SEARCHING FOR YOU. HOMED IN ON YOUR WARNING BEACON.
WE'D BETTER GO.
YUH-YEAH...
GOOD. WE'VE IDENTIFIED THIS SYSTEM AND ITS RELATIVE POSITION TO CYBERTRON.
ALMOST THERE. CAN YOU TRANSFORM?
SO...
...WE CAN GO HOME. AT LAST!
HOME.
I LIKE THE SOUND OF THAT!

STARSCREAM

INTRODUCTION

Starscream's list of priorities begins and ends with 'me.' While other Decepticons fight because they see the bigger picture or to satisfy some need for chaos, Starscream is utterly focused on his own personal advancement; whatever head-count he amasses on the battleground is just to make the powers-that-be sit up and take note. Ultimately, Starscream sees himself taking Megatron's place as supreme Decepticon commander, but is wise enough to know that a direct challenge is out of the question. However, should someone else succeed in toppling Megatron, Starscream will be there in a flash to fill the power vacuum.

HISTORY

BEST OF ENEMIES

As much as one needs to watch one's back when around Starscream, he too needs to keep a wary optic out over his shoulder. The list of Decepticons Starscream has trampled and shoved aside to get where he is is extensive, and still-to-be-settled grudges are plentiful. Starscream is rarely first into battle, but is always at the head of queue when it comes to taking the credit. Case in point, the battle of Ky-Alexa during the early days of the campaign for control of Cybertron. Though it was largely Barricade who finally broke the back of the long siege at this key Autobot stronghold, it was Starscream who demonstrably claimed the territory in the name of the Decepticons, picking off any last pockets of resistance from high altitude.

ROBOT MODE

Starscream is an expert in the art of the fast and deadly attack, typified by his lightning lunge – a sudden burst of coiled, hyper-reactive cydraulics and musculature that results in him springing forward too fast for most optics to register.

Starscream also has a dedicated flip-out launcher assembly, shoulder-mounted and equilibrium balanced, allowing for tremble-free single shot targeting and elimination.

SCALE RELATION CHART

WEAPONS MODE

Starscream's extensive arsenal of hunter missiles is accessible in both robot and airborne mode.

Laser guided, the missiles can independently lock into multiple targets simultaneously and launch in (airborne) clusters.

The thermo-reactive warheads burn at over 1000 degrees centigrade on impact, slagging all but the densest metals.

VEHICLE MODE

Starscream's aerial mode (on Earth, a modified F-22 Raptor jet fighter) is supremely fast and manoeuvrable.

He can literally brake in mid-air and use his reinforced wings as battering weapons, or just blow enemies from the sky with air-to-air laser guided missiles.

Sophisticated navigational equipment allows him to fly no matter what the conditions, even at ultra-low level.

STARSCREAM

THEIR WAR! OUR WORLD!
YOUR COMIC!
FREE PLAYING CARDS!
TRANS FORMERS
ROBOTS IN DISGUISE
DECEPTICONS RULE OK
ON SALE NOW!
AWESOME NEW COMIC STRIPS FEATURING THE GREATEST TRANSFORMERS CREATORS!
UNBELIEVABLE PRIZE GIVEAWAYS!
FREE GIFT with EVERY ISSUE!